THE PARALLEL MAN

Richard Purtill

DAW BOOKS, INC.
DONALD A. WOLLHEIM, PUBLISHER
1633 Broadway, New York, NY 10019

Cover art by Ken W. Kelly.

DAW Collectors' Book No. 587

First Printing, July 1984

1 2 3 4 5 6 7 8 9

PRINTED IN U. S. A.

"Can it be that all this is just some sort of spell cast over me the last two years, when Mortifer came with his warning of the firedrakes? I never trusted him. What did he do, kidnap me and imprison me here? The kingdom . . . my father . . . are they. . . ?"

I swallowed a lump in my throat and faltered. "In some of the old tales they say that men taken under the hills by the elvish folk have returned to find their friends grown old or dead; that a year with them under the hills is many years in the world of mortals. Is it something like that?"

Droste's eyes met mine as he said, "As nearly as we can tell from the time of your last genuine memory until now is about five hundred years."

RICHARD PURTILL
in DAW Books:

THE GOLDEN GRYPHON FEATHER

THE STOLEN GODDESS

THE MIRROR OF HELEN

THE PARALLEL MAN

Part I

1. Beyond the Broken Sky

The firedrake screamed as it swooped at me again. I lifted my shield and felt the blistering heat on my shield arm as the fiery blast of the creature's breath flared out. After a moment I dared to flick the shield aside and swing my sword with all my strength at one of the fiercely beating wings. The sword bit into the leathery membrane, but it was almost wrenched from my hand when the firedrake half folded its wings and dropped like a spent arrow into the abyss below us. I leaned back against the tree, letting my weary arms drop to my sides. There would be blessed moments of rest while the creature swooped even lower to build momentum, then spiraled upwards with beats of those mighty wings to where I stood on the ledge. The massive old tree protected me from a thunderbolt-like attack from above; the creature had to swoop by almost level with me, trying to burn or claw me.

Behind me I heard the clink of a chain as Princess Delora tried to move farther into the crevice which gave her a little shelter from the side-blast of the firedrake's breath. I risked a quick glance over my shoulder. Her lovely face was grim as she met my eyes. She knew and I knew that no Champion had successfully defended a Sacrifice from the firedrake since the sacrifices had begun years ago. Worse yet, I, her defender, was the one they called the Afflicted Prince. If the Falling Sickness struck me now. . . .

I didn't dare to worry about that, or let myself think about what might happen if I lost consciousness as I leaned over the edge to see the firedrake's position. It was flying a little awkwardly, I saw with a stab of hope, taking longer to fly up to the ledge than it had last time. If I could only injure that wing more the creature might not be able to fly strongly enough to make its way up to the ledge if it had to swoop down again. There would be more glory in killing it, but I would be content with a draw which would allow Delora and myself to spend the prescribed time on the ledge and be released with honor.

The firedrake was on a level with the ledge again but instead of swooping at me it banked, spilled air from its wings and landed at the other end of the ledge. Then it began to advance toward me with a shuffling motion of its hind legs. The wings were poised over its back and the forelegs with their vicious claws were making striking motions in the air. But the real danger was the writhing serpentine neck which could send the blunt head at me with the force of a battering ram; even without the wicked teeth in the gaping mouth or the fire that the creature could breathe, that head could knock me flat, my bones shattered. The tree would be no obstacle; the creature could strike around it from either side.

I stepped toward it along the ledge, my shield poised to ward off another fire blast, ready to leap back if the head darted toward me. If the creature could kill me or knock me off the ledge, nothing could prevent it from continuing its inexorable progress down the ledge to the crevice where Delora was chained and making a grisly feast on her helpless body.

The neck straightened, a sign that the creature was about to let loose another fiery breath. If I stood and took the blast on my shield, the firedrake could bound toward me and be on me before I could recover. With desperate invention, I hurled my shield at the gaping jaws and dived under the head toward the more vulnerable body. I heard my shield crunch as the firedrake instinctively snapped at it; then I was lunging for the creature's heart with my extended sword.

The tip penetrated a hand's breadth and then would go no

farther. My feet scrabbled for purchase on the stony ledge, but the creature was wincing back, its fore claws trying to tear the sword from my grasp. I felt the hilt slipping from my sweat-slippery hand: in a moment, the creature would spit out the shield and I would face its jaws and its fire with neither sword nor shield. Only one thing to do: I let go of the sword and grasped the neck above me with both arms. I swung my legs up and wrapped them around the neck and with a desperate heave and pull got myself on top of the neck. I reached for my heavy dirk, tore it from its sheath and plunged it into the firedrake, above my head. Then using the dirk as an anchor, I heaved myself toward the creature's head. The fiery breath whooshed out in a useless reflex. I was behind it now and hardly felt the heat, but a muffled cry from Delora told me that the crevice had not sheltered her from the blast.

Now I was straddling the neck, just behind the firedrake's head. My dirk plunged into one of the creature's eyes, stuck for a heartstopping instant, then came out. Now the other eye: the firedrake was blind. The worst moment was when I had to let go and drop from the monster's neck; I almost froze to the false security it offered. But I was hardly on the ground before the firedrake battered its head against the mountainside, trying to knock off whatever had stung it so intolerably. I would have been smashed to a pulp, and still might be; I huddled in the angle between the ledge and the mountain wall that rose above it.

The firedrake shrieked again and again; the pain in my ears was excruciating. Gobbets of black oily blood spattered the ledge as its head thrashed back and forth. My sword was still stuck in its breast. Did I dare make a dash for it? If only the creature would blunder off the ledge. But no, it was going forward, toward Delora, extending its wings to guide itself by the pressure of the right wing against the mountain wall. Only one way to save Delora from the fiery blast that would surely come: I rolled toward the ledge's rim and sprang up at the firedrake's left wing, tearing at the leathery membrane with my dirk as I hung on the wing with all my weight.

The massive head came around toward me with the speed of a striking serpent, and that completed the overbalancing I had hoped for. The firedrake began to topple from the ledge, carrying me with him. Delora was safe; as for me, perhaps the harpers would find another name than "Afflicted" to remember me by. Firedrake slayer: a good name to die with, if one must die.

Of course I cherished mad hopes; perhaps I could cushion my fall on the creature's body or leap free into the trees below. But I think I would have died there—if the sky had not broken. Impossibly, fantastically, as I began to slide over the edge clinging to the firedrake's wing, a jagged circle opened in the sky above me; shards of blue rained down from it. Beyond the circle was what looked like a gray corridor, as if the sky was a wall with a passage behind it. In the corridor, men in strange, skin-tight garments that covered all but hands and faces. Gods? Demons? But surely neither would show the blank amazement, the utter incomprehension with which they looked at me and at the firedrake.

A convulsive shudder by the firedrake sent us over the edge and we tumbled crazily as the creature beat its one sound wing in an effort to fly. Then something seized me like a giant invisible hand and the firedrake tumbled on below as I began to rise in the air toward that mad circle in the sky. A scream came from below: Delora's nerve had cracked at last at this final insanity. My dirk was still in my hand and I brought it up with some instinctive thought of defending Delora or myself against the strangers. Concerned faces looking down at me from the hole in the sky suddenly became wary. One of the men pointed some stubby object at me; there was a strangely familiar purple flash and I lost consciousness.

I awoke in the strangest room I had ever been in. The walls and ceiling were the color of thick cream, featureless and smooth. One wall shone with a cold clear light and on one of the other walls an oval patch of colors moved in slowly swirling patterns. I was lying in a bed, covered with some sort of pale, clinging coverlet, feeling the sick shaken sensation that often came to me after an attack of the Falling Sickness. It often helped to get up and move around, so I tried to fling aside the coverlet to rise from the bed. The coverlet would not release me; it clung to the bed and to my body with firm but gentle persistence. There was no discomfort, but I was trapped in the bed: my blood began to pound and my headache grew worse as I struggled to get free.

As if in response a white circle appeared on the wall opposite the bed, the size of a shield and about head height. At first it was featureless, then suddenly a woman's face appeared in it, not like a picture but solid and real, yet with nothing but the face visible, framed in a sort of white haze. The eyes looked as if they saw me. The face gave a small, impersonal smile and a soft voice said, "Someone will be with you in a moment." Then the face vanished and the white circle faded.

I had no way to measure time, but the time that followed seemed to me longer than a "moment" by any reckoning. Finally a white rectangle, like a door, appeared on the wall. At first it was merely a shape of light, then suddenly it was an opening in the wall and people were walking through it into the room. One of them was the woman whose face I had seen. She was dressed in a skin-tight white garment that covered everything but her face and hands; around her waist was some sort of belt from which hung a number of small glittering objects. Somehow she reminded me of the chatelaine of a castle with her bunch of keys at her belt, though the glittering objects looked not at all like keys.

Beside her was a man dressed in a black garment which did not cover his head and seemed somewhat looser than the woman's. There were touches of white at his neck and wrists and his thin, intense face was that of a scholar or a monk. Behind the man in black and the woman in white were two men in very similar garments, one in brown and one in gray. Something about the way the man in gray carried himself made me look more closely at him. He had the crude features and vacant look of a serf but instead of the usual shock of hair he seemed to be wearing a curious kind of skullcap of bright blue which covered his head to just above the eyebrows.

The man in brown was no serf; he did not have the intensity or authority of the man in black but he looked competent and responsible. He was pushing some sort of gray box in front of him; I blinked as I saw that it seemed to hang suspended in the air with no support. I did not want to face these strangers flat on my back; I tried to heave myself up and found that the bed changed its shape to support my back. I still felt at a disadvantage, confined as I was by the clinging coverlet, but at least I could face my visitors. I folded my arms and made my face impassive, waiting for them to make the first move.

The little group stopped at the foot of my bed and I suppressed a smile as I realized that it was they who were at a slight disadvantage; the bed was a high one and I looked down on them like a ruler from his chair of state. The man in black inclined his head gravely and said in a deep voice, "I am Justinian Droste, of the Citizens' Liberties Union." The title meant nothing to me; some sort of guild perhaps, though the man did not look like a merchant.

"I am Casmir," I said shortly, "of Castle Thorn." The gear they had taken from me would tell them that I was a knight of Thorn, if they had skill to read the markings, but it would be foolish to name myself as the Prince to men who might be enemies.

The man who had named himself Justinian Droste hesitated; he looked somehow unsure of himself; perhaps even embarrassed. "There are things which you will learn," he said, "about the place you call Castlethorn." He ran the name together as if he were unfamiliar with it, but that might be a deception. "That place is not what you believed it to be," he went on, "and you have been used by others for purposes of their own. That is over now and I am here to safeguard your rights."

I tried to keep irony out of my voice as I said, "I thank you for that, Ser Droste. Tell me then, since you are my . . . guardian . . . am I a prisoner in this place or a guest?"

The woman in white broke in, "This is a hospital. You're here because of some injuries you've suffered and for observation. When we're sure that you're able to function normally you'll be discharged." A hospital; the word was unfamiliar but perhaps it was a sort of hospice. A place of healing at any rate. The woman in her form-fitting white garment did not look like a sister of charity, though I supposed she must be something of the sort. I gave her what I could manage of a bow from my position in the bed and turned back to Droste.

"And then?" I asked.

"You will be quite free to do as you wish," he said, a little too smoothly. "In fact one reason for our presence here is to formalize your rights." He beckoned to the man in brown, who pushed the gray box to the right side of my bed. I looked closely at it; I had not been wrong, it did float in the air. "Please place your hand on the Register," Droste said. The floating box was an uncanny object, but it would be unfitting to show fear before them; I placed my hand on the box without hesitation.

"Please give your name," said the man in brown. I did hesitate then—was this some sort of oath taking? Their gray box meant nothing to me and I could not be oathbound just by saying my name.

"Casmir of Thorn," I said and couldn't completely conceal my start when a smooth neutral voice seemingly from within the box said "Casmir F. Thorn." There was a tingle on my wrist and I took my hand from the box to find a green dot about as large as the tip of a finger glowing on my wrist. I picked at it and found that it was a thin patch of some smooth material which came away easily enough from the skin of my wrist, but then stuck to my fingers.

"Your citizenship and credit chip," said Droste, "honored anywhere in the Universal Commonwealth. Wear it wherever on your body you like; most people find a wrist most convenient.'' He pushed back the cuff to show a blue dot similar to my green one on the back of his left wrist.

The woman in white pulled away the hood which covered her hair and showed me a green dot on the lobe of her ear. ''Move it around occasionally,'' she said, ''it can irritate the skin if it stays too long in one place.'' I put the thing back on my wrist; there would be time to investigate it further when I was alone. The woman in white turned to Droste. ''We'd better go now,'' she said. ''The medication causes him to need considerable rest.'' To me she said, ''Try to relax and please don't fight the clingsheet, as you were doing after you woke up. It's there to keep you from injuring yourself while you're healing, but we'll have you out of it soon.'' I sketched a bow again. It was irksome to be confined but I needed to know more before I took any action. She smiled politely but without warmth. ''We're short of human staff but I'm leaving the andro here for you. Tell him if you want anything.'' The serf with the odd skullcap looked at me vacantly, then at a gesture from the woman went and stood near the opening through which the party had come into the room.

Droste inclined his head to me in his curiously formal way. ''You must have many questions,'' he said. ''Be patient. They will all be answered.'' He turned to go.

''There's one question I'd like answered now,'' I said. ''Before I . . . woke up here . . . there was a woman with me; she may have been injured. Is she in this place too?''

Droste looked at me with an expression I could not read and said with curious gentleness, ''No . . . no. We did not bring a woman from where we brought you, Casmir of Thorn.'' He must have seen from my expression that I was not satisfied and he went on after a slight pause. ''There was no woman with you when we found you. No woman at all.'' Then he turned and left the room, followed by the woman and the man in brown. The doorway filled with white light which faded to show an apparently unbroken wall, as blank as the gaze of the blue-capped serf who stood against it.

2. The Room of Enchantments

My first impulse was to get free of the clinging coverlet, overpower the serf and ransack this place for any sign of Delora. But I forced myself to be patient. My earlier struggle with what the woman had called the clingsheet had caused the woman's face to appear on the wall: the enchantment that made the thing confine me must also give some warning of attempts to escape it. Nor did I know the spell to make the door appear in the wall, and it was not likely that the serf did either. If I could get the woman in here alone. . . . Best wait awhile until the men had gone about their affairs. And I was inexplicably weary. Better rest a little and gain strength. I lay back and the bed subsided to a level position again. . . .

When I awoke the room was nearly dark, and someone was moving about behind me. I lunged upward and again the bed folded up to support my back. The light became bright again and the person behind me came into view; a woman in a white garment like that the other woman had worn. But this woman's face and hands were a rich dark brown. Perhaps she had painted herself like some of the barbarians, or had some disease? But the skin looked healthy and normal.

The woman gave a smile which despite her strange appearance had a good deal more warmth in it than the smile of the other woman in white. "Feeling more rested?" she asked. "I'm Molly, your night nurse."

I smiled back at her. "I had thought that I was beyond the age for a nurse, Lady. I am Casmir, a man of Thorn."

She laughed with a flash of white teeth. "Perhaps they don't call us nurses on Thorn. Sisters perhaps, or medics? I'm a prentice Healer, I care for people who are sick as part of my training. Is there anything I can do for you?"

She looked friendly and it was worth trying. I plucked at the clinging coverlet. "This grows irksome." She walked to the foot of the bed, touched it with a glittering object she took from her belt. She looked intently at something I could not see for a moment then nodded.

"Yes, I think we can take you out of the clingsheet now, Casmir. Move carefully at first; you had some broken bones and some second-degree burns and your body is still finishing its job of healing." She touched my coverlet with another glittering object and I was able to push it away and swing my legs over the side of the bed. My legs were bare but I was covered well enough for decency in some sort of short tunic of fine white cloth.

I slid cautiously to the floor; I was weak, but I have been weaker after an attack of the Falling Sickness. The dark-skinned woman named Molly watched me carefully but did not interfere as I took a few tentative steps, stretched and touched my toes. "Any dizziness?" she asked.

"Less than usual," I said. Molly looked at me with brilliant dark eyes, but said nothing. I went on slowly, moved by an impulse I did not fully understand. "Since I was a child I've had what we call the Falling Sickness. I . . . lose consciousness . . . especially at moments of stress. I've injured myself before when I've had an attack while riding or climbing. I'm no stranger to Healers."

The dark-faced woman frowned in a puzzled way. "There's nothing on your chart to indicate epilepsy," she said. "Let me look at your admission records." She went to the foot of the bed and touched it again with one of the objects from her belt. Glowing letters and numbers appeared in a square near the center of the footstand, as if some invisible scribe were writing them there. They disappeared and intricate and mysterious traceries of lines took their place. "No, there's nothing organically wrong," she said. "But there's scarring on the nerve paths. The last time I saw scarring like that was on the chart of a criminal who'd had repeated run-ins with the monitors. Someone has used a neural interrupter on you, often enough to leave nerve scars."

I looked at her without comprehension. "A neural . . . ?"

She raised her eyebrows. "Well, there are nicknames for them: 'stunsticks,' 'rupters,' but that's the standard name. Monitors use them—police, peace officers. They'll render a person unconscious for a varying period of time, depending on distance and intensity. Normally they don't do you much harm, but then most people are never exposed to them even once. But repeated exposure can cause confusion and memory loss due to scarring. I see that they have you on Lysergol to repair the scarring."

I frowned at her, trying to untangle her meaning from the unfamiliar words she was using. "You are saying that I have no sickness, that I will not lose consciousness as I have done in the past . . . ?"

She smiled reassuringly. "Not unless someone uses a neural interrupter on you again. In fact, right now, even that wouldn't do it because the Lysergol prevents the . . ." Her voice trailed away and her eyes looked over my shoulder to where the serf still stood by the wall. I kept my face impassive, but my heart leaped. If I understood her aright, some enchantment they were practicing on me prevented the action of the spell that would make me unconscious. That was why they had the serf standing by, to overpower me in case of need. They would learn their mistake in time, but I still needed to know more before I acted. Nor, if I could avoid it, did I want to injure this woman in my escape. At the moment it would be best to distract her, if I could.

"I thank you, Lady," I said. "You are kind, though your face is strange to me. In my land there are none who have skin the color of yours. It is . . . ?" I paused and she laughed.

"Yes, all over," she said in reply to my unspoken question. "I'm from Thopia; we were settled by people from a place here at Home they call Africa, where the people are mostly my color. Are all of your people big and blond like you?"

I smiled at her. "Many more are fair than dark, and none dark of skin," I told her. "Dark women are much admired, for they are rare."

She laughed. "I'll have to visit your planet," she said. "Is Thorn the . . ." Just then one of the glittering things at her belt gave a small musical sound. "Damn, I have to go," she said. "The convenience is in the corner there, and if you don't know how to key anything you need, ask the andro to do it. Don't overtire yourself. I'll look in again when I can, but it may not be until tomorrow." With another flashing grin, she walked to the wall and touched it at a place where there was a small circle outlined with a gray line. There was first the rectangle of light, then an opening which she walked out of. The corridor beyond the door seemed featureless in the glimpse I got of it before the opening became a rectangle of light and vanished.

In the direction Molly had gestured when she mentioned the "convenience" there was another gray circle on a blank wall. I touched it and though it did not yield or seem to change, a white rectangle appeared next to it and in an instant became an opening. Beyond it was a small square room with a basin and a covered garderobe. When I pressed circles of various colors at random, water came from some remarkable places and in a variety of temperatures and I emerged from the "convenience" feeling considerably refreshed but somewhat bemused. That I was in a nest of enchanters was evident, but I had not known that enchanters lived so luxuriously.

I was now feeling hungry and decided to see what orders the serf would obey. "Bring food," I told him. He gave me a vacant stare but moved over to another part of the wall and pressed yet another circle. One of the now-familiar white rectangles appeared and became an opening into a niche in the wall which contained a covered tray. The serf brought it out and walked over to a place near the bed. He touched a circle on the bed itself and a table and chair rose from the floor. He lifted the cover from the tray and stood back.

The beverage in the cup was bitter but hot and the food was good enough, though without much taste to it. When I had finished, I went about the room looking for circles to press. There were not too many more; one turned on some sort of chute for disposal of trash and another opened a cupboard with fresh tunics like the one I wore. I took the opportunity to change my garment, but when I tossed the soiled one to the serf he sent it down the disposal chute. I shrugged; it was a waste of gear, but the gear was not mine.

There were no more circles on the wall, but there were several on the headboard of the bed. One pair of circles increased or decreased the light from the glowing wall when you kept your finger on them. Another seemed to have no effect at first but I glanced up and saw that the colors swirling in the oval on one wall had changed. I almost lifted my finger from the circle, but suddenly the swirling colors gave way to what seemed to be a window. I saw blue sky with clouds and a curiously shaped range of mountains. I lifted my finger from the circle and went closer to the oval; but when I touched it the surface of the wall still seemed to be there. Suddenly a movement in the scene revealed through the oval caught my eye; what looked like a tiny human figure moving at the base of one of the mountains. Suddenly my eyes made sense of scale and proportion; those were not mountains, but monstrous buildings, each larger than Castle Thorn, ranged in rows beside broad roads. On the roads moved curiously shaped objects and an occasional walking human figure, but no horses or other beasts. I seemed to be looking at the scene from a great height. Was this a window or some illusory scene produced by enchantment?

I gazed for a long time but learned little. From the light it seemed early morning and not much went on outside of the monstrous buildings. I wondered if I was in truth inside one of them, looking out of some window high above the ground. Finally I went back to the circle which had produced this scene and touched it again. Sky and buildings vanished from the oval and I seemed to be looking into an adjoining room, where several people were carrying on a conversation. The room was richly, if oddly, decorated and the men and women in it were dressed in bright and intricate garments which hugged some parts of their bodies, left other parts bare and fell in rich folds in other areas. They were talking in an oddly cadenced way so that their voices wove in and out like a part-song, and though I understood most of the words I could make little sense of what they were saying. I watched in puzzlement for a while then touched the circle again.

The oval showed a rushing mountain stream while sweet strains of music filled the room. I began to see that this was some magical toy; the oddly dressed men and women had been performing some masque or mummery, while this peaceful scene with its accompanying music was another sort of entertainment. I touched the circle again and found myself gazing into another, more quietly decorated room where two women reclined on couches and talked. They were dressed in close-fitting garments, one in blue and the other in brown, and I saw the gleam of one of the little colored circles on one woman's wrist. I settled on the bed to watch this scene for a while; it seemed to offer some hope of learning something of this place I had found myself in.

Suddenly one woman's face almost filled the oval, larger than life; you could see tears in her eyes. Then it was as if you were looking through a hole in the wall into the room again, but from a different angle. At first the sudden shifts made me dizzy, but gradually I began to see a sort of sense to the changing images; it was as if you saw through the eyes of someone in the room with the women, who now went closer to them, now stepped away, now changed his position with respect to them.

The women continued to talk, and a serf with the same odd blue skullcap that the serf in my room wore brought them cups of some beverage, then left the room. Gradually their talk began to make some sense to me. They were speaking about a man named John who went away on some sort of journey; they spoke of him as "flitting." One of the women was John's wife or lover; she was worried because in John's absence she had "gone into red." This seemed somehow connected with the circle of color on her wrist, which was red instead of being green like mine and like the other woman's. The other woman seemed sure that John would not be angry for a while after he returned. They began to speak of love and I grew weary of them; I touched the circle on the bed again and the oval showed only a swirl of colors again.

I lay back on the bed trying to make some sense of what I had seen. Enchanters, I knew, could call up visions, indeed my tutor, Mortifer, had called up visions for me as part of my education. But I was no enchanter and I had called up these visions by merely touching a circle drawn on my bed. Indeed, even the serf had touched one of the circles to get my food and another to dispose of my soiled tunic. Some of these enchantments seemed to work for anyone, even a serf. Others seemed to need the glittering objects which Molly and the other woman wore at their belts.

I felt that I knew enough to escape from this room and begin my search for Delora, but I would rather do so without raising an alarm. Best go soon before day came and brought more people to deal with. . . .

I cursed as a white rectangle appeared on the wall and became a door. Had I left it too late? But what came through the door was another blue-capped serf; he turned to the one already in the room and said, "Report to Central and wait for orders."

The serf addressed shook his blue-capped head obstinately. "Orders to stay here," he said.

The new serf said in a low voice, "Override Argent. Report to Central." The other serf slouched out the door, which vanished as before. I tensed my muscles; might as well hit this new jailer before he got fully oriented.

He was pulling something from the waist of his gray garment and stepping toward me with strangely unserflike quickness and alertness when I launched myself at him. His hand came up holding something and there was a purple flash, then my shoulder hit him in the midrift, and he went over backwards, his head hitting the floor with a satisfying thunk. I was on top of him in an instant, my hands poised to strike, but there was no mistaking the flaccid sprawl of his limbs; that rap of his head on the floor had knocked him out.

Something about his head was odd; surely I hadn't cracked his skull? No, it was the blue cap, slightly askew. I pulled it off, a thin cap of metal, curiously flexible. Under the cap was short-cut hair and the face, on closer examination, was not the face of a serf. Whoever this man was, he had been masquerading. What he could do, I could do. I bent over his body, trying to solve the fastenings on his gray garment. These were simple enough; a touch at a circle on the collar and the garment opened down the front and I was able to peel it off of him. The stuff it was made of stretched easily and I was able to draw it onto my body without trouble. Another touch at the circle on the collar and the garment closed itself again.

The man wore underlinen not unlike the tunic I wore and I began to wonder if I could pass his unconscious body off as mine for a while. Something had rolled away when I hit him. A little searching revealed a stubby object like the one which the man had pointed at me from the hole in the sky. One end was rounded, but the other was a dull jewel which was disquietingly familiar. Surely Mortifer had carried a jewel like that . . .

No time to worry about that now. The thing fitted easily into my hand and one of the now-familiar circles was near my forefinger. The man on the floor was beginning to stir a little; I extended the object toward him and touched the circle. There was a purple flash and his body went limp again. I looked at the object in my hand with distaste; what use would valor or skill at arms be against an enchantment like this?

For the moment though, it served my purpose well enough. I tucked it into a sort of pouch at the waist of the gray garment and heaved the inert body of the man who had originally worn the garment onto the bed. I flung the coverlet over the lower part of his body and moved his limp arm so that it concealed his dark hair as much as possible. I pressed the circle on the wall and held my breath until the white rectangle appeared and became a door. Then I put the blue cap on my head and stepped out into the corridor, trying to imitate a serf's shambling gait and vacant stare. For better or worse I was out of the room and must face the unknown dangers at the place of enchanters with what wits and courage I could muster.

3. Under the Dome

As I stepped into the corridor the first thing I saw was a long gray box, unpleasantly like a coffin, floating in the air at about the height of my waist. When I put my hand on its end it began to glide down the corridor, but as soon as I removed my hand it stopped. There was a circle about halfway down the length of the box. I touched it and the lid of the box sprang open, revealing a narrow interior which seemed to be padded. I touched the circle again and the lid closed. I had an unpleasant feeling that this box had been planned to receive my body after I had been rendered unconscious by the weapon now tucked into the pouch in my garment.

A great deal depended on what enchantment had been put on the box. If it had to be guided to its destination I was at a loss, for I had no idea of where to go now that I had left my room. But perhaps the spell on the box would lead it to some destination where I might learn something more about this trap in which I found myself. I placed both my hands on the end of the box and followed it as it glided off down the corridor, trying to remember to shamble and stare like a serf, for there were cross corridors ahead and someone might come upon me at any moment.

At the first cross corridor the box swung left, which gave me hope that it was under some spell to bring it to a definite destination. I was in a broader corridor now; an unfamiliar woman in a white garment was approaching me. Her eyes flicked over me without interest as those of a lady of the court would flick over a serf carrying some burden through the castle. I heard footfalls behind me and a man in brown overtook me and walked past me without even a sideways glance.

A little farther down the corridor there was a large circle on the floor. The box glided to the center of this and then stopped. I risked a glance around; surely this was not our destination. Then the whole area of the circle flashed white and vanished. I almost jumped free, but I could feel something solid under my feet; I was floating rather than falling downward. We floated past several corridors like that I had come from and then stopped. The corridor I was now in was wider and a little dingier than the corridor I had come from and to my excitement there seemed to be just a breath of wind and a smell of fresh air in it. When the box started to glide off again I stopped it by taking my hands off of it and took the jewel-nosed weapon from my pouch. Holding it below the level of the box in my right hand I put my left hand on the box again and it glided off.

The breeze grew stronger. The box, with me following, rounded a corner, and there was an open door a dozen paces away. Beside it lounged a thickset man in a green garment, who called out softly, "Any trouble?" I shook my head, keeping my face down as much as I could so that he saw mostly my blue-capped head and a foreshortened face. The box approached him with nightmare slowness; pushing at it seemed not to hurry it at all. I saw his eyes narrow and his hand go to his belt. "Hold on," he said. "You're not . . ." I raised my right hand above the level of the box and pressed the circle on my weapon. There was a purple flash and the man crumpled, astonishment on his face.

I wanted his garment and I wanted to hide his body, but the corridor was unpromisingly bare. Suddenly I grinned. Stripping his garment from him, I touched the circle on the box, bundled his body into it and shut the lid. Immediately the box floated off out of the open door. While I stood staring it turned a corner out of my sight. I heard a sort of click, then a rumble, and when I moved to peer cautiously out the door a black cart of some sort was vanishing down the road with no beast to draw it. I shrugged, bundled the green garment under my arm and set off down the road in the direction opposite to that which the cart had taken. The spell on the box must work either by weight or by contact with living flesh, I thought; once a body was inside it the box would probably float to its destination with no one touching it from outside.

I half regretted not following the box all the way to its destination, but it would have been easy for me to be trapped by my ignorance in a situation which I could not fight my way out of. For the moment it was enough that I was free, had a change of disguises and a weapon. That was little enough for a stranger in a land of enchanters, but it was a start. Eventually I must find out what had happened to Delora, but if she was in the building I had just come from she was probably being treated no worse than I had been; she could wait until I knew more and had more powers at my disposal.

I looked up at the monstrous bulk of the building I had just left. I had discarded the thought of going from room to room looking for Delora as soon as I had realized the size of the buildings in this wizards' city. I felt like an ant crawling among the benches of the Great Hall as I looked up at the towering shapes around me. The broad street on which I walked had raised walkways at each side but there were no animal droppings on the road between the walkways; I remembered that I had seen no beasts of burden in the view of the city that the oval had shown me.

There was a cross street ahead of me; I slowed my shambling walk and stayed close to the side of the building. When I rounded the corner I stood and gaped as I have seen serfs do. I would gladly be rid of my present disguise but until I was I had better act the part. There were a few people walking on the street, clad in close-fitting garments of various hues so that it was hard to tell women from men at a distance. This street was less sterile than the one I had just left; a row of trees bordered the roadway on each side. There were a few doorways with writing above them which I could not read at this distance; some of them might be shops.

About a bowshot down the street a little knot of blue-capped serfs stood in a ragged line, gazing vacantly around them. I walked toward them slowly trying to gauge the dangers and advantages of joining them. Among them I would be inconspicuous, but if they were some sort of work party I might find myself led off to labor at some task which I could not escape from without arousing suspicion. A howling sound from the street behind me made up my mind; it sounded as if it might be some sort of alarm call. I shambled to the end of the line of serfs and tried to imitate their vacant stares.

The howling sound grew louder and down the street rushed a glittering thing as large as a small cottage, flashing lights and making a growling sound. I think that if I had been wearing a sword I would have drawn it and my hand crept toward the weapon in my pouch, though much good it would be against such a monster. But the thing, whatever it was, turned at the corner and went down the street I had just come from. The howl ceased abruptly; at the rate the thing had been moving it should have just about reached the door I had come out of.

Something else was coming down the street, a sort of platform with seats on it which floated a few handsbreadths above the street. It moved slowly and almost silently with only a low hum. The platform stopped near the little group of serfs and they began to climb aboard it. I hesitated and then followed them; that howling device might have nothing to do with me but if it did I wanted to be clear of this area before it returned, perhaps to track me down with unknown enchantments. The size and speed of the thing had shaken me a little; against a thing like that what could a warrior do?

The platform seemed to need guidance as little as the gray box had; it threaded its way down street after street until I realized uneasily that I would be hard-pressed to find the building where I had been held. I began to look for a chance to jump off of the platform, but the streets were too wide and clear and the speed of the platform had increased.

Just as I was beginning to wonder if I should jump anyway the platform turned into a set of gates and we were going through an area of grass and small shrubs; not ideal but the best chance I had seen so far. I leapt and landed on my feet, letting my momentum carry me forward so that I made a rolling fall first onto my feet, then onto my hip, then onto my shoulder, as my old arms-master had taught me. I jumped to my feet and looked toward the moving platform to see if my leap had caused any disturbance. To my dismay a shortish, stocky serf had leapt after me and was picking himself up from the ground; his leap had been much more awkward than mine.

I shot a glance at the platform; it was sweeping around a bend out of sight. Whether the serf had come after me out of dim-witted imitation or was some sort of overseer who was chasing me down, I didn't want him trailing after me. I ran toward him, ready to strike him while he was still off balance. "Wait," he cried, and the voice did not sound like that of a serf. "Wait, I'm on your side."

I stood poised within striking distance and said grimly, "And what side is that?"

He grinned at me and spread his hands out at his side as if to show his peaceful intentions. "Let's say the underside, cit. If you're desperate enough to masquerade as an andro you must be so far into the red that you're infra, or else you're in a lot of bother with the Structure. I'm in some bother myself; let's help each other."

I looked at him appraisingly. Now he had dropped his serf mannerisms; he looked cocky and confident, but also a little shifty. If he were a soldier under my command I would suspect him of slacking and keep my eye on him but if I wanted some home comforts stolen or scrounged on a campaign he would be the man I would pick for the job. I kept myself in position to strike, but let him see me relax a little. "How did you find me out?" I asked.

He smiled with a touch of patronage. "Ah, I'm an old hand at this, cit, I have my ways. Most people, they see the blue dome and they don't look at what's under it. You could cross your eyes and stick out your tongue and then they'd never notice. But once you know that a man can play andro you begin looking. The monitors look too, and they have some nasty ways of finding out if you're what you seem. Too many thieves and wilders try to hide under the dome. Now you don't look like a wilder and if you're a thief I can probably offer you better pickings than you'd find yourself. What do you say?"

I pretended to hesitate, but I had already made up my mind. This man wanted to use me for some purpose of his own; by going along with him for a while I would have help and protection which I would have trouble getting in any other way. That he would try to use me and abandon me I didn't doubt; I must keep my wits about me and drop him just before he was ready to drop me. "What do you offer me?" I asked.

He grinned, sure he had me hooked. "Ecus, cit," he said. "Extraplanetary credit units, good anywhere in the Commonwealth, don't go through your chip. Spend 'em here near the starport or use 'em for star passage and see the Universe. Ever flitted, cit?"

"Don't ask too many questions," I said, "and we'll get along better. What do I have to do for all this?"

He looked around us as if the shrubs might conceal listeners and said in a conspiratorial mutter, "There's this woman I work for, d'you see? Half mad and more than half bad. Always out for more of everything than she has any right to. Right now she's got a scheme that needs someone to play the part of her rich cousin—a real ultraviolet—who hasn't spoken to her in years. Told me to go out and get an andro, an andro like *me* she said, to do the job. I'm never quite sure if she knows what I really am and just enjoys treating me as an andro or whether she actually believes that a real andro can do the things I do for her. Anyway I set off looking for an andro *just* like me; somebody hiding under the blue dome. Been riding around with work parties most of yesterday and all night. Just about to pack it in when I spotted you. You weren't bad but you exaggerate a little too much; common beginner's mistake. Didn't even have to chase you; you got right on the mover with me. Thought I'd lost you when you made that dive though."

I looked at him consideringly. Despite the strange words, I had understood his story fairly well and I could see no purpose in his telling it to me if it were not true. It seemed that I would have to assume another disguise, with the advantage that this time I would have helpers, who for the sake of their own plans would help my masquerade. Best to say nothing, though, that might seem to pledge my honor to his plans. "Well, perhaps we can help each other," I said. "Where must we go to find this lady of yours?"

He laughed, sure that he had bent me to his purpose with his vague promises. "Why up the road we were traveling on," he said. "I told you that I had given up. Those andros are on their way to Flavia's place now. Even she can't get humans to wait on her guests, but she dresses andros up as near like humans as the laws allow and sometimes a bit nearer. All we have to do is go up the road and in the back way; if it wasn't for your dive we could have ridden in comfort."

I was glad nevertheless for the longish walk up the road that followed; it gave me time to think out plans. My companion kept up a stream of complaints and comments at first but he soon ran out of breath. If this encounter had done nothing more it had shown me the dangers and the restrictions of posing as an "andro" as these folk called their serfs. I needed a disguise that would give me more freedom of movement and with luck I was about to have such a disguise served to me on a salver.

The house, when we came to it, was a poor enough place to have such extensive grounds, hardly more than a pavilion.

Tables were set on the lawns and the blue-capped serfs I was beginning to think of as "andros" were moving among them, clad in a curious variety of costumes, all of which included some sort of head covering which almost, but not quite, covered their blue caps. They were setting out food and drink on the tables, and I realized that I was hungry. The meal I had eaten in the room I had escaped from was less than I was used to eating.

My companion led me round the corner of the pavilion, knocked somewhat perfunctorily at a translucent panel and then slid it aside. It was the first more or less normal door I had seen since I awoke in this land of enchanters. Inside the panel was a large, untidy bedroom dominated by a huge bed. In the bed, propped up against multi-colored pillows was a small, frail woman with faded blond hair and a sharp-featured, discontented face. She said in a fretful voice, "Is this creature the best you could find, Pello? Well, it will have to do. You," she said to me, "come here. Forget your designation and your former assignment. You are going to dress as a human and impersonate my cousin Fenric. Obey no orders but mine. This is a . . . a joke. It is not against your directives. Understand?" I inclined my head, not knowing how to address her. "Let me hear your voice," she snapped.

"Yes, Lady," I ventured.

She looked at me with narrowed eyes. "You might do," she said. "Don't talk any more than you can help. Look down your nose at people. When someone's as rich as Fenric people put up with almost anything, so if you're asked a question you can't answer just ignore it. For the Mercy's sake don't talk about hunting; Fenric is mad about it and you'd give yourself away in a minute to anyone who knows anything about it. Part of your getup will be a fake chip that looks like a high violet; don't try to use it or you'll give everything away. For emergency use Pello will give you some ecus, enough to make a good display. Don't dare to lose them; they're a good portion of my credit for this period."

She lay back against the pillows and shut her eyes. "Take it away, Pello, and dress it. Make sure the wig and makeup over the dome is undetectable."

The man called Pello led me out of the room by a different sliding door; this one led into an interior corridor. A glance back over my shoulder showed me that the walls of the bedroom seemed transparent from within; the woman's bed might have been sitting on the open lawn before the house to all appearance. A curious fancy, to sleep in an interior room that seemed to be out in the open.

As we walked down the corridor, Pello spoke in a low voice. "She knows that you're a masquerading human all right; no one could expect a real andro to obey orders like that. But she keeps up the pretense, curse her, so she can treat us like andros; it satisfies some spite in her. You've probably guessed my plan; take the clothing, the fake chip and the ecus and get away from here at the first opportunity. Once we're clear we split the ecus. You can go your own way or stick with me. Simple enough, eh?"

I nodded slowly. "Too simple, perhaps," I said. "You say she knows that you're not an . . . andro, and that I'm not either. She doesn't look foolish or trusting to me. Why is she trusting us?"

Pello smiled wolfishly. "She thinks she has us trapped here," he said. "It's easier to get in this place than it is to get out. But I've been here long enough to know all of her little ways; not just the ones she knows I know, but those she thinks I don't." We came to another door which he slid aside and I followed him into a small room with clothing laid out on a couch. Pello picked up a richly ornamented belt and stroked it with a curious smile on his face. "This belt for instance. If you left the grounds wearing it this thing would tear you in two. If you didn't wear it Flavia would notice and take other measures. Unless . . ." he opened a slit in his gray suit and pulled out a belt which seemed identical to that on the bed. "Unless," he concluded with a sly smile, "you think one step ahead of her. Now let's get you dressed."

I touched the circle at the collar of my gray garment and stripped it off, then lifted the blue cap from my head with a sense of relief. With Pello's help I put on a close-fitting suit of sky blue and a vest, boots, and short cloak in darker blue, decorated with silver; the belt matched these and a pouch went at the belt. As he helped me dress and fix a violet-colored circle to my wrist, Pello talked. "Flavia needs backing for her trading ventures," he said. "It costs a great deal to live in this style, and though she's shrewd she's been unlucky. It's the old story; you can't get credit unless you don't need it. If her cousin the ultraviolet Fenric is visiting her and appears on good terms with her the local syndics will think that she only has to ask him and he'll back her. They'll fall over themselves trying to get in first, though if they thought she was in trouble they'd try to bring her down and carve up her trade among themselves."

This meant little to me except to give some rough sort of sense to the masquerade I was undertaking. I could still see one objection though: "Does no one here know this Fenric, then?" I asked.

Pello shook his head. "He hasn't been Home for so long that anyone who did know him wouldn't recognize him. Anyway, a man that wealthy has no friends, only hangers-on and toadies. Fenric spends most of his time on a big tract of wilderness on some primitive planet, hunting every kind of animal he can import. His money comes from something that needs no work; some sort of monopoly in star-trade I think. So he plays at being a lord and ignores the Commonwealth."

"He's a sort of prince then, this Fenric?" I asked, and Pello shrugged and nodded. I smiled then and threw back my cloak over my shoulder. If they wanted someone to play a prince, I was better suited for the part than they knew. And though this clothing was strange, I felt more myself in it than I had done since I woke in that strange room. With a smile still on my lips, I followed Pello out onto the lawn where a crowd of brightly dressed men and women had gathered. My eyes swept over them indifferently and then suddenly I checked my stride and stared. For there, among the chattering crowd, surrounded by a circle of men and women and laughing with them at some jest, was Princess Delora!

4. The Hunter

Delora was dressed in a long, flowing garment of unfamiliar cut and her hair seemed longer, but her face and her mannerisms, such as the little toss of her head she gave when she laughed, were just as I remembered. Yet, when her eyes met mine across the crowded lawn there was no recognition in them. Her glance passed over my garments and perhaps she noticed the glint of the violet circle on my wrist which, according to Pello's rambling, marked me as a man of wealth and consequence. She gave me a little smile before turning back to her companions and that smile shook me. It was full of an insincere warmth I was used to from court ladies who coveted the importance my attention could give them. There could be many reasons for Delora to pretend not to know me, to conceal her surprise at seeing me, but none I could think of for her to give me a smile full of such professional coquetry.

I moved toward her, and the people on the lawn fell back respectfully as courtiers might have done at Castle Thorn. It strengthened my resolve to act as I would have acted in my own place; when I came up to the group in which she was standing I turned to the oldest man among them and said to him pleasantly but with authority, "You may present this lady to me."

He gave a little bow and said with dignity, "My honor, sir. Holder Fenric, may I present O Dela Delora, who graces our Living Theater with her beauty and talent."

She gave a delicately exaggerated curtsy and smiled up at me with a professional charm that Princess Delora had never needed to learn. But her husky voice was the same as she said, "One has heard of you, of course, Holder."

I inclined my head to the man who had introduced us and said with a dismissive note in my voice, "My thanks, sir." He faded away tactfully, taking the others with him, and I turned to this new and puzzling Delora. "Your face seems very familiar," I said.

She pouted with an annoyance that seemed genuine. "I don't see how that can be, Holder," she said, "since I understand that you haven't been Home in some years. We of the Living Theater guard our images rather carefully. One wouldn't want to be confused with those who perform for the 3V, whose images are, well, a bit too common. Theater people even have a prejudice against having holos taken."

"And yet," I said, "I'd swear that you have a tiny and entrancing mark on your arm, right . . . here!" Taking her right arm gently but firmly I lifted it so that the sleeve fell back and revealed a little red crescent-shaped mark on the inside of her upper arm; Delora's clan mark. If it had not been there I would have felt and looked a fool, but I had to know. I released her arm and looked into her eyes, hoping for some spark of recognition; that mark had swept away all my doubts that this was really Delora.

But there was only anger and fear in her eyes; she stepped back and said, "A man of your wealth, Holder, may buy a good deal, including, it seems, some rather personal information. I don't know what you hope to gain by this, but I would call your behavior Uncivil. I am not without . . ."

The voice of Flavia interrupted her, "My dear, is Fenric playing one of his little jests on you? He teased me unmercifully when we were children." I felt clawlike fingers on my arm and looked down to see her at my side, her sharp features exaggerated by a hairdo which made her hair float like a soft cloud and an elaborate dress more suited to a woman younger and more beautiful.

The woman who had been introduced to me as Dela Delora hesitated, then decided to make light of her annoyance. She gave a little trill of laughter which seemed quite natural but went on an instant too long. "All right, Flavia, I admit he got a rise out of me. I'll leave you two to renew childhood memories. Come and see me, Holder—in my new play." She smiled a little too sweetly and moved away.

Flavia's voice was sweetly acid as she said to me in a low voice, "You've evidently studied the behavior of real ultraviolets; you seem just as convinced as they that the world revolves around you. Not a soul here doubts that you're Fenric. Now keep your mouth shut and that supercilious look on your face while I flaunt you at my guests." She led me toward the crowd around the tables and began presenting her guests to me. I behaved as badly as I'd always dreamed of doing at receptions and parties; snubbing everyone who seemed self-important or unpleasant, talking only to people who interested me. Gradually I gathered a little circle around me; several of the women who were intelligent as well as beautiful, several of the men who seemed to be of some weight, and an outspoken old woman who was as amused by me as I was by her.

I disengaged my arm from Flavia's and gave her a little push. "See to your guests, cousin dear," I drawled. "I'm quite happy here." She gave me a look of baffled fury, but she had no choice but to go. Presently Pello appeared at my elbow with a tray containing small tidbits of food and a flagon of good wine. He was dressed in a costume that was not as extravagant as those of the real andros; if he got rid of his blue cap he could pass for one of the guests. "Stay here with those things," I told him and he bowed with a little glint in his eye and filled my cup.

A youngish pleasant-faced man who had not said much so far broke into the slight pause as I sipped my wine. "Heard that you hunt a bit, Holder," he said.

I could almost feel the tension in Pello as he held out the tray for me to select another tidbit. "Been known to, yes," I told the pleasant-faced man.

"Benton's my name, Holder; you wouldn't have heard of

me but I do a bit in that line myself. Got a bit of land up in the hills," he said. The colored circle on his wrist was the same shade as mine and his wealth presumably was genuine. He went on: "Thing is, we used this new process they've discovered to clone and culture some wild boars. Got the cells from a museum exhibit. Well, they're established now, but none of my people is too sure how to hunt them for the best sport. They've dug up some history books; tell me that boar were hunted from horses at one time . . ."

I shook my head. "Can be done but it takes a long time to train the horses and if the country is hilly they're not much use. Better on foot anyway. Have you got proper boar spears? They'll come right down the shaft at you if you don't have a cross-piece . . ." We were soon absorbed in highly enjoyable technical discussion and the rest of the circle gradually drifted away, smiling indulgently.

Eventually, as I had hoped, Benton said tentatively, "Don't suppose you'd like to see my place. Not much by your standards, I know, Holder, but any time you'd care to . . ."

"Call me Fenric," I said. "Why not now? These people are beginning to bore me."

Benton's face lit up. "Would you really like to? Be delighted. Only came to this affair to meet you if I could. Have a little craft down on the meadow yonder. Anything you want to bring?"

"Can always get new stuff," I said. "Oh I know," I turned to Pello and said, "Get another tray of those things and another jug of the wine and bring them along." He shot me a glance of startled admiration and trotted off to do my bidding. "Oh, Flavia," I called as I saw her in a group nearby. "I'm off with Benton here for a while. Call on me if you need to on that matter we spoke of, but I don't see why you'd need to, perfectly sound proposition, you'll find the money easily enough. Expect me when you see me." And I strolled off with Benton, Pello trotting behind us with a loaded tray, leaving Flavia open-mouthed. She couldn't quarrel with me or threaten me in public without destroying the illusion she had gone to such pains to create, and anyway I thought that she had gotten good value for the pouchful of little golden tokens at my belt.

Benton's "little craft" might have been a small pavilion erected in the meadow, but when we entered the door it lifted smoothly into the air and began moving away from the monstrous towers of the city. I turned to Pello. "Put that tray down somewhere and get that blue thing off your head," I told him. "You can report to me later." I turned to Benton. "Sometimes useful to have a man about who isn't noticed *as* a man," I said blandly.

Benton stared and then laughed. "By the Mercy, you star traders are high-handed," he said admiringly. "That breaks about sixteen laws here at Home and there are plenty who'd call it Uncivil. But I can see the advantages. A violet chip can expose you to all sorts of unpleasantness at times."

An inspiration struck me. "Been meaning to speak to you about that," I said. Opening the collar of my garment I reached in and peeled from the green "chip" which I had been given soon after I woke in this land from my underarm, where it had been hidden since I donned the gray suit of the false andro. I put it on my wrist and transferred the violet chip to where the green one had been, hoping that whatever stuck the false chip to my skin would hold it there. "Now I'm away from Flavia's I prefer not to be known as Fenric. The name that goes with this one is Casmir Thorn. So far as anyone is concerned I'm here to advise you on hunting boar."

Benton seemed genuinely shaken. "I didn't know it was even possible for a private citizen to have a second chip," he said. "Of course you hear stories about Commonwealth agents being given false identities but . . . you don't do a little work for the UC on the side, do you, um Casmir?"

I smiled at him. "I don't like lying and I don't like refusing to answer questions from a friend," I said. "The less you ask me the less I'll have to do either." Benton laughed and shrugged, but there was admiration in his eyes; whatever explanation he was imagining for my mysterious activities was evidently creditable to me. I was quite pleased with myself; at one stroke I had cut away the immense complication of pretending to be a wealthy man of whose real life I knew nothing. I might still betray myself by my ignorance in conversation with these folk, but I did not have to keep up the character of Fenric.

As it turned out, I need not have worried. Young Benton was an enthusiast of hunting and was glad to talk of nothing else. For a knight of Thorn, hunting is part of the yearly round; one of the things that is done in season, for food and to exercise the skills of hand and eye that a knight needs. As the prince, I had been expected to take the lead in hunting as well as in war, and older and more experienced men had quietly made sure that I knew my business. I had heard plenty of hunting stories, for that was one of their ways of teaching, and I had myself taken most of the kinds of birds and beasts that are counted worth hunting: deer and wild pigs for the table, of course, but also beasts of the warren: wolves, foxes and wildcats, badgers, martens and otter, even squirrels and hares. And, of course, I had hawked for hares and for game birds.

There is a skill to taking each of these beasts, and my teachers would not have counted me a hunter if I had not known each of these skills. Benton seemed to know little of such skills, except for the most elementary sort of tracking; his talk was all of hunts in which he had put his life at risk against large and dangerous beasts, including many whose nature I could only guess at from details he let drop in the telling. Of course a hunter must have courage; a stag may turn at bay and boars are notoriously dangerous and unpredictable. But battle, not the chase, is the place to demonstrate bravery; skill is what counts in the hunt.

In fact, I was growing a little weary of Benton's stories, for an armed and skillful man is in little real danger from a brute beast. But then he said something which changed my mind. Looking around the richly furnished room where we sat on cushioned chairs while our magical craft flew high in the air, Benton said hesitantly, "Most of my friends think I'm a bit of a fool to spend so much time and credit on hunting, you know. But it seems more . . . more real than most things a man can do these days. Just your own skill and a few primitive weapons against, well, against Nature. No machines to do it for you, to get between you and the thing you're doing."

Remembering the giant towers, the broad sterile streets with their few trees for show, thinking of weapons which made a man unconscious with the pressure of a finger, I began to realize that the hunt would have a value for these enchanters which a man of Thorn could scarcely understand. If they went to war it would probably be with strange wizardries which would leave little room for strength or bravery. I smiled at Benton and said, "You'll be glad enough of a spear between you and the boar; a full-grown tusker can rip a man from knee to breast and lay him stark dead with one stroke. Have these beasts been hunted at all yet?"

Benton shook his head. "Not these; they're just out of the tanks not long ago. But we managed to salvage some memory chains from the beast in the museum exhibit. Don't know if you've followed the techniques they're using these days for memory recovery from dead cells. They reckon that by what they call mix and blend techniques they can create quite a good facsimile of the original memory, with some artificial memories mixed in. Of course they'd only really know if they tried it on humans, and the Citizens' Liberties Union would be after them if they tried that. Not to say it hasn't been done in secret, of course."

"Ran across a man named Droste," I said as casually as I could manage. "Justinian Droste, I think, who had some sort of connection with that group."

Benton grinned. "Oh yes, Droste is quite a big noise here

at Home, though you may not have heard of him. Always on the 3V or in the latest fax, complaining about someone being deprived of their rights.'' He laughed. ''Been looking a bit silly today, though. Had a big case built up against some scientist for experimentation on humans. Then his star witness or chief exhibit, the man who was the victim of the experiments, disappeared. Without him Droste has no case. Joke is Droste's own principles are getting in the way of looking for the man. Since he's a citizen he has a right to privacy. They can't even broadcast a holo of him, only appeal for him to come forward. Droste claims the man's been kidnapped, but his evidence isn't too strong. For all anyone knows, he just got tired of the food at Central Receiving and decided to check himself out informally.''

Most of this was meaningless to me, but at least it assured me that Droste was a man of some note, who could be found if I wanted to find him. Since Droste seemed to know something about how I had come to this city of the enchanters, I might have to seek him out eventually.

I was tired enough of his hunting tales to pretend more interest than I really felt. I made some noncommittal noise, which encouraged Benton to go on. ''Story just broke,'' he said, ''but it should be in the fax by now. Let's see.'' He touched something on the arm of his chair and from a slit in a low table by his side came a thin sheet of some flimsy parchment-like material, covered with writing. ''Ah yes, here it is on the first sheet,'' said Benton, ''with a backup on another sheet, which I'll key if you're interested.'' He handed me the sheet, which was covered with writing in small square characters which it took me a moment to master, though I am a fair scribe. In large letters at the top of the sheet were the words, ''CLU Head Accuses Academician,'' then my hand clenched on the sheet, crumpling it in involuntary betrayal of my emotions. For under those words were two pictures, more vivid and lifelike than any painting I had ever seen in church or castle. One showed the face of Justinian Droste looking much as I had seen him from my bed soon after I awoke. The other face, staring out at me from the picture with a familiar saturnine glower, was that of my tutor and guardian, Mortifer the Enchanter!

5. Benton Hall

After the first shock, it almost seemed inevitable. Mortifer was an enchanter, I was in a land of enchanters, so surely he must have played some part in bringing me here. I had never entirely trusted Mortifer, despite my respect for my father, who had trusted the enchanter so well that he set him over me as my tutor and guardian. Despite his outward suavity and respectful air, Mortifer had always struck me as a cold man who regarded other people only as pieces in some elaborate game. Perhaps he had brought me to this land to play some part in some game of his; well, he would find me an unwieldy tool. I remembered that as a youth I had sometimes outwitted better players at board games by moving my pieces about almost at random and letting them wrack their brains to discover the elaborate stratagems they thought lay behind my moves. I was doing much the same in this deadlier game, keeping on the move and in disguise, hoping that one of my random moves would lead to some advantage for me.

Benton had not noticed my agitation, for he was intent on another sheet of the same kind as the one he had handed me. "Doesn't really say much," he complained. "The backup is all details on the careers of the two men and the original story didn't say all that much either, just hints that Mortifer had been caught more or less red-handed experimenting on humans and that Droste had the alleged subject of the experiments. Then there was a late break saying that the man had disappeared, with Droste all but accusing Mortifer of kidnapping or worse."

"This Mortifer," I said as casually as I could manage, "from where does he come, of what Academy is he a member?"

Benton chuckled. "By the Mercy, you're right. If a man's an academician there must be an academy about somewhere. Well, let's see, must be on the fax here somewhere. Ah yes; Royal Academy of Life Sciences of Carpathia."

I nearly blurted out that if there were any "Royal Academy" in the land of Carpathia, I, the Prince Royal of Carpathia, should know of it; but I restrained my tongue. Whatever lies Mortifer had told he had at least used the name of my homeland in those lies and this gave me a reason to put the question I was burning to ask: "And where is this place Carpathia?" I said, keeping my voice as steady as I could.

But Benton's answer made little sense. "One of those little star systems out on the Tail, I think," he said with a shrug. "One terranorm planet which went pretty well back to nature during the Wars of Unity. Fairly flourishing place, now, I believe—reasonable amount of trade. Would have thought that you'd know more about it than I, since you're a star-trader. Shouldn't be more than a few days' flit from Home in a modern starship."

He was looking very slightly puzzled, a puzzlement that might turn to suspicion, and much as I longed to press my questions I shrugged and turned the conversation to his obsession, knowing that it would distract him.

"Ah well," I said, "can't remember everything. I've forgotten already how many boars you told me you had." He was off at once on questions and stories about hunting which lasted until his flying pavilion came to earth with a very slight jarring sensation. Out of politeness, I had not even been able to read further on the lettered sheet he had given me, but I folded it and shoved it in my pouch for future reading.

The flying pavilion was grounded beside a sort of lodge, a rustic enough place but with some dignity. There were blue-capped serfs to meet us at the door and, to my joy, a blazing fire on the hearth in the great hall. Benton smiled at the pleasure I did not try to hide. "Try to keep up the old ways here," he said. "I'd like you to try some of my venison, if you're hungry, and some Napa I have laid down here." I agreed heartily since only the edge had been taken from my appetite by the snacks served at Flavia's gathering. A table was set for us before the fire, but we had hardly begun to eat when a slim green-clad figure appeared at the entrance hall, obviously feminine, despite red hair cut like a boy's. She had a bow in her hand and a dagger at her belt. Benton rose to his feet with a smile. "Mirianne," he said. "Nice to see you up here. Mirianne, this is, er, Casmir Thorn. Casmir, my sister, Mirianne, who laughs at my hobby but drops in on me when she needs a change from her usual pursuits."

"Pursuits is right," said the girl. "Nice to be the hunter instead of the hunted for a change. At least the men you bring up here are interested in hunting animals rather than heiresses—usually. But welcome to Benton Hall anyway, Casmir Thorn." Her eyes met mine as her fingers rubbed the violet-colored circle on her earlobe in a gesture that seemed unconscious, but may have been meant to give point to her words.

I grinned at her; there was something rather engaging about this forthright young heiress. "Why lady," I told her, "I am not here to hunt for an heiress, only for a little sport with your brother's boars. But I can see the attractions of—nobler quarry."

She laughed at that, and fell into easy conversation with her brother and myself. I asked what sport she had found with her bow, and from that the talk turned to archery. Before long we were shooting her hunting arrows at targets here and there in the hall, as men will do sometimes in a hunting lodge after the evening meal when no ladies are present. Here the lady was the worst of us, and crowed with laughter when we lodged an arrow in the mouth of a deer head hung high on the wall or shot a shaft into the opening of a wine flagon held presented toward us by a serf. There is a knack to this kind of indoor shooting, usually done with the bows at half-pull and I can usually put an arrow where I want it every time in such games, though at real shooting out of doors I do not rank with the best. By the end of the evening Benton and his sister were well pleased with me for slight enough reasons, and I went to my bed well pleased with the evening and with their company.

In the morning we broke our fast with bread and sweet preserves, along with a hot bitter liquid that was refreshing once you got used to its wry taste. Benton showed me his arms room and I belted on a short sword and dagger, feeling foolishly relieved to be armed again, though I knew that edged weapons would be of little use against the enchanter's weapons I had seen. Benton had spears of various patterns and I showed him the right length for a boar spear and where to place a cross-bar. Benton summoned a man in brown, who carried off the spear and returned surprisingly quickly with several made to the same pattern but with cross-bars.

Carrying the spears, we set off down the hill upon which the lodge was built to look at the thickets where the wild pigs had established themselves. Benton had whistled up a dog, which seemed more a pet than a hunter and Mirianne had her bow and a quiver of hunting arrows, but it was more an amble and an exploration than a hunt. As we reached some broken ground, small hillocks overgrown with underbrush, Benton hesitated. "There's a sonic fence along here," he said, "and the beasties we're after are inside it. We're not really prepared . . ." Just then the dog by his side began to bark noisily. Then, his excitement growing, the beast sprang from Benton's side to chase something that scuttled away in the underbrush. "Oh damn," said Benton, "he's got a neutralizer in his collar; he's right through the fence. Ranger! Come back here, you idiot!" He ran forward, shouting and whistling, with Mirianne and me at his side. For a second I had a feeling of panic, then felt a sort of vibration deep in my bones, but in a stride I felt normal again.

"If you hadn't spoiled him . . ." Mirianne had begun when there was a sharp yipping sound and the dog ran back toward us, his tail between his legs, followed by a long lithe form that was chillingly familiar.

"Young tusket," I told my companions. "Most dangerous kind. Keep your spear pointed at him." I fell into a guard stance, tracking the boar with my spear-head, my hands in position on the shaft to thrust or take the shock of an impact. An old boar will stand his ground and threaten, a sow is usually dangerous only when she is defending her young, but a young boar is as dangerous as he is unpredictable.

This one slashed at the dog, and then, as I had feared, swerved toward us. "Spread out," I called to the others. Mirianne was carrying a spear and I had to treat her as a hunter, not as a lady to be protected. With the three of us to choose from, no longer in a clump but spread out in a line, the young boar hesitated. If he wanted to run between us and escape, I for one would let him; I had no need for meat or trophies and here among strangers I had no reputation to maintain. A prince must be first in the chase, as in all things, but a private person may choose not to compete.

The best thing would be for the boar to attack me; I could dispatch him with the skill of long practice. The worst would be for the boar to go for Mirianne; she had spirit but even if she had the skill she did not have the weight to stop the beast. Neither the best nor the worst happened; the boar went for Benton. "Shoulder," I shouted and he shifted the aim of his spear-head from the head, an almost impossible target, to the shoulder. The spearpoint skidded over the rough skin of the boar, then caught, and pierced through the ribs just behind the left foreleg. If the boar had the cunning to swerve away from Benton it could simply run off the point and be free to attack again. But with the insensate fury of its kind it tried frantically to reach the target it had picked.

As it scrabbled its way toward Benton the spear pierced its internal organs, but it must have missed the heart, for the creature's strength seemed unabated. When it reached the cross-bar its full weight bore on Benton for the first time; he staggered backwards a few paces. "Down," I cried, "ground the spearbutt if you can." It would have been best if he had thrown his weight at the boar, almost as if he were as eager to get at the boar as the boar was to get at him, but that was not something I could explain in a few shouted words. He did almost as well, though, by bearing down with his weight on the spearbutt until he had got it lower than the point which was deep in the boar's guts. Helped by a small hillock behind him he grounded the butt and let the boar pump out its blood and life against the unyielding toughness of the spear.

I had been ready to run full tilt into the boar's side with my spear if Benton had not held him, but now I relaxed a little, shifted my spear to my left hand and drew my shortsword. So long as Benton was holding him all was well. If Benton weakened I could hamstring the boar and end it. Mirianne moved up beside me, pale but in control of herself. She looked at the thrashing boar with horrified fascination, but she neither shrank back from it nor gloated at its overthrow. My liking for her increased and I gave her a quick smile. "Almost over now," I told her and then called to Benton, "Shall I finish it for you?" He gave a jerky nod, as his muscles still strained against the boar's struggles, and I darted in, grabbed a foreleg and flipped the boar on its back. A quick hard slash and the throat was cut. Blood flowed; the limbs thrashed more slowly and stopped. There was a stink of death as muscles relaxed. I grinned at the exhausted Benton. "Now you know how to kill a boar," I said.

He stood up, working his cramped fingers. "By the Mercy," he said, and it was half a prayer and half an oath. He smiled at me and said with fair pretense of jauntiness, "Thanks for letting me have this one. But if we meet another one today, I think I may let you kill it."

I shook my head. "The boar chose you. And you did very well for your first. Next time bear forward with your weight and try to use the leverage of the spear to get the beast off its feet . . ." I went on with my advice until he had recovered his breath and his composure. Then I tactfully urged him toward the lodge, on the pretext of sending serfs back for the meat. If I judged him correctly, Benton's courage was of the sort that rises to meet a challenge, but leaves the man shaken afterward. I remembered young knights with that temperament, vomiting after a battle, their bodies taking revenge for the strain that had been put on them.

When we arrived back at the lodge, Benton left Mirianne and me with a murmured apology. Mirianne turned to me and said in a low voice, "Thank you for what you did; and for what you didn't do. He's too hard on himself in many ways, but I think that for once he feels he's done well. I don't know what you are, Casmir Thorn, aside from being a very cool and professional huntsman, but if we can do anything for you . . ."

I smiled at her and said lightly, "At the moment I could do with a change of clothing and to have my man, Pellow, found and sent to me."

"Of course," she said. She looked at me searchingly, then touched my arm lightly and went on into the lodge. I found my own room and stripped off my garments and relaxed in a stream of water in the "convenience." It was a pleasure; it would be easy to get used to and I wondered if something of the sort could be devised at Castle Thorn if I ever got back there.

When I had dried myself on towels that looked rough but were marvelously smooth, Pellow appeared at the doorway, carrying an armload of clothing. He looked at me with an enigmatic expression and laid his burden on the bed. "From the lady of the house," he said. "You're in high favor it seems. I've been evading questions about you; my ignorance was taken for great discretion. Apparently you really do know about hunting. If I hadn't seen holos of him, I'd begin to think that you were really Fenric."

I smiled grimly. "Hunting is probably the only thing that Fenric and I have in common," I said.

Pellow looked at me speculatively. "Here at Home and on most planets I know of hunting as an amusement for the very wealthy," he said, "and yet the C and C chip of yours looks plain, ordinary green to me. Or is that a fake too? And if it isn't, what in the Mercy's name were you doing under that fake blue dome?"

I looked into his eyes which were a dark gray. "Suppose you tell me your story first," I said. It would be a lie of course, but the sort of lie it was might tell me something about the man.

He looked down at his hands, then looked into my eyes again with a good imitation of candor. "My name is Joseph Pellow," he said. "Pellow with a 'w.' I was a starflitter once, but I got into trouble on a Szilar planet and the lizards got me Banned. Took my free ride Home and squandered the ecus I'd been paid off in trying to forget my Banning. Tried to get more and only got into trouble. Finally, the only thing for it was to go under the dome. What I want now is to get out to one of the newer human colonies. Things are too rigid here at Home; no scope for an enterprising man. With my share of the ecus in that pouch . . ." His eyes flicked over to where I had left my soiled clothing.

I hid a smile and picked up the belt with the pouch. Opening the pouch I spilled out the small gold-colored discs it contained and told Pellow, "Divide them into two piles; I'll choose one and leave you the other." He gave me an admiring grin and did as I had told him. I watched his hands to see that none of the discs disappeared.

"Benton can't stay here much longer," he told me, "he has business to attend to in the City. He'd leave you here to hunt if you wanted, but I wouldn't advise it; you're too isolated here if the Fenric thing blows up, as it might. You have quick wits and good luck, cit; I'll be happy to stay with you if you want me. What are your plans?"

I looked at him and said slowly, "Stay with me if you wish, Joseph Pellow. I plan to make a journey, if I am not prevented. A journey to a place called Carpathia."

6. The Voyage of Argo

Pellow darted a sharp glance at me. "And where may that be?" he asked.

I tried to remember the exact words that Benton had used. "One of those little star systems out on the Tail," I said.

Pellow's hands closed protectively over his little pile of golden discs. "Star passage is expensive," he said. "Still . . . Wait, though. Benton is a trader. Surely he can arrange passage for us if you ask him. From the questions the sister asked me, they have the idea that you do some sort of secret work. If you told him that you wanted to get to Carpathia unobtrusively, he'd probably be able to arrange passage for us on a cargo ship. It's done often enough; I know from my days as a flitter."

I hesitated. Some obscure sense that I was somehow being pursued or sought told me to leave no trail that could be followed. But surely if Benton thought that I was on some secret errand he would turn away anyone trying to trace me. I had done little enough for him but he felt himself obliged to me. In fact, I felt the obligation went in the other direction, but I liked young Benton and did not mind being obliged to him. "All right," I said reluctantly, "I'll speak to him."

Benton was engagingly eager to do something for me and to prove himself a man of importance. He unlocked a small room full of gleaming machines and flashing lights, spoke to several disembodied voices and imaged faces, then turned to me and said with a smile, "We're in luck. A startrader who owes our House a favor actually has a cargo going to Carpathia.

You and Pellow will travel as special supercargoes responsible for that shipment. The ship is a little Independent carrying a variety of small shipments. But the captain is experienced and the ship is fairly new. She'll lift day after tomorrow if that suits you, and you can go aboard tomorrow night." He waved my thanks aside and plunged into plans for a boar hunt and feast the next day.

Between the hunt and the feast I was in little condition to take much note of my surroundings when Benton's flying pavilion carried me back to the city the following evening. The pavilion landed on a broad sweep of what looked like lawn, brightly lit by glowing globes on tall poles. When Pellow and I emerged from the pavilion, though, the stuff underfoot was not grass, but some slightly resilient stuff the color of grass. A tough, competent-looking man in dark, close-fitting garments met us and led us past immense mysterious structures to a great circular thing like a giant's shield flung carelessly on the false greensward. A square opening in the edge of the thing was evidently an entryway; a light warmer than that of the globes spilled from it.

I could see as we entered that the outer walls of this thing were immensely thick, made of some smooth dark stuff. Inside there was a sort of high desk occupied by a slender man with the look of a clerk. On the wall behind the desk the word "Argo" was written in golden letters and beneath it a stylized picture of a small sailing galley that might have sailed the Inner Sea. Standing beside the desk talking to the clerk-like man was a tall dark-haired woman of remarkable beauty, who had an air of absolute authority. She might have been a reigning queen. I was not surprised when my guide saluted her and said, "These are the two men from Degnan Freres, Captain."

She nodded and gave us a brief smile which lit up her dark eyes. "I'm Elena Petros," she said. "Welcome aboard *Argo*. Your cargo is already sealed in Gamma hold. I'm not sure what point there is to sending you with it, but you're welcome enough to the spare cabin." Her eyes flicked over

Pellow, then measured me with an approving look I might have resented from a woman less magnificent than this one. "You have the look of a Carpathian," she told me. "I presume that you're homeward bound."

A sudden feeling of uncertainty swept over me. "I hope so, Lady," I said. Could it really be so easy as this, stepping onto this strange vessel and voyaging back to the place I had come from? Could Castle Thorn and the court of Carpathia exist in the same world as this place of enchantments? Young Benton had spoken as if a cargo to Carpathia was a commonplace enough affair, but surely nothing like this great dark disc had ever been seen in the skies of my homeland.

Captain Elena Petros looked into my eyes. Her own magnificent dark eyes seemed to pierce my soul. "Will home be home when you get back?" she said softly. "Yes, it's a feeling that starflitters know well." She gave another of her brilliant smiles and turned to the clerkly man. "There shouldn't be anything else coming aboard tonight, Tamma," she told him. "You might as well seal the sally port and show these cits to their cabin." The man saluted and slid down from his high stool. He touched a circle on the desk, and with a deep hum the ramp by which we had climbed up to this entryway lifted from the ground, pivoting on the threshold. It covered the doorway by which we had entered, fitting flush with the inner wall with a slight click. Those thick walls and the door made by the ramp made a formidable barrier. Against what, I wondered?

I learned the next morning, as I sat on my bed in a room that except for its smaller size might have been the room I had awakened in in the place they had called a "hospital." As in that other room, there was an oval of swirling colors on the wall, which Pellow called a "View." Touching one of the now-familiar circles made the colors vanish, to be replaced by what seemed to be a window looking out on the area we had walked through the night before. Dawn was still streaking the sky with colors when three red flashes chased each other across the scene and a woman's voice spoke from the air. "Lift off in thirty seconds," said the voice. "Off-duty crew and passengers secure for liftoff."

There was a deep rumble and the fabric of the room shook very slightly. In the oval view the ground suddenly dropped away, and I saw again, as I had seen from Benton's flying pavilion, the towers of the enchanters' city. It was set among rolling hills: I looked for Benton's estate and lodge but we were soon too high to see any building of ordinary size. Higher and higher we went: I saw snow-capped mountains off to one side and a blue infinity that could only be the sea a long way off on the other side. The panorama was already vaster than any I had seen from the highest peak in Carpathia, but we rose yet higher; what sky I could see turned strangely dark, and the land beneath me seemed to take on a curve. As I watched in fascination the arc of the sky grew in proportion to the land and stars began to appear. After I don't know how long I saw the starry sky engulf the land and sea, until the place we had come from was only a circle of misty blue set in a night sky full of stars.

Pellow's voice brought me out of my trance. "Spectacular, isn't it?" he said softly. "We take off on gravity-effect engines and it's most economical to head straight for the sun, so you see the whole dayside." Then he said more briskly, "There's time for breakfast before we go Q. Not that you'll feel the lack of it when you're Q-time, but your body needs it and you might as well eat while you can still enjoy it." From a niche in the wall very much like that in the "hospital" room he produced a tray of food and drink far tastier than the food in the "hospital" had been. Pellow grinned. "Trust a Greek captain to see that the Departure Day breakfast is a good one," he said.

The three flashes came again and the voice said, "Prepare to go Q." Pellow shrugged and carried our dishes back to the niche where they were whisked away as if by invisible fingers. A whooshing sound as of a great wind sighed through the room for a moment and Pellow cocked his head to listen. "Letting air out of the cargo holds," he said. "The captain leaves it till the last moment for some reason. Wonder what the cargo is that we're supposed to be in charge of.'' He went to his bunk and stretched himself out, turning his face to the wall. Three flashes again and the disembodied voice said, ''Entering Q space.''

In the View the starry sky blinked out, to be replaced by a curious gray blankness through which amorphous gray shapes moved slowly. After a moment I tore my eyes away and turned my face to the wall as Pellow had done. Waves of hot and cold seemed to move through my body and I had the unpleasant feeling that those gray shapes were moving unseen through the room and through my body. My heart pounded, then seemed to stop and start again. A weight seemed to rest on my chest and I struggled for breath, then the weight vanished and I was panting in shallow breaths. My sight blurred, then cleared again. Gradually I settled into a sort of dull apathy, as if my body and my emotions had been worn out by the rapid oscillations of sensation, and had retreated to a dumb quiescence.

Pellow lifted his head and spoke in a dull monotone. ''The first few minutes are the worst, after that your body overloads. You won't feel like doing anything, but it's important for you to move around, and take some nourishment when it's provided, otherwise it's worse when you come out of it. You can let yourself go during what would be the sleep period so long as you're able to rouse yourself at the change of watches. It will seem like three or four days until we come out of Q and you'll feel about as you do now for five or ten days afterward, unless you take some steps. I can help you there; starflitters get to know a few tricks . . .'' His voice trailed off and he stared dully ahead of him.

''What is this . . . this . . . state?'' I asked him. Pellow gave the ghost of a shrug.

''I'm not sure anyone knows, really,'' he said. ''We go outside of normal space and time, into—this. We call it quasi-space and quasi-time, Q space and Q time for short. We come back into realspace an immense distance away from where we started. Carpathia is twelve zir from Home; light takes about fifty odd years to make the journey. So far as anyone can tell the ship has taken no realtime at all to make the journey. If you could go Q near a planetary mass starflits would be a great deal easier. As it is, you have to get about fifty diameters out from your departure planet before you can flit and your point of arrival has to be a long way out from any planetary mass. We may take as much as a day or two realtime from POA to planetside. But we'll still be in emotional freeze—we won't care."

Indeed, I cared for little in the time that followed, or seemed to follow. But I forced myself to activity, mindful of Pellow's warning. I did endless exercises, which never seemed to raise a sweat or leave me tired, forced myself to rise from the bed promptly at the bell which marked the change of watch, and made myself swallow the tasteless food which appeared in the niche in our cabin. On a long campaign I have been so tired that I fought and marched and choked down food like a man asleep yet walking; this was like those times except that I felt no weariness, only a dull apathy that made it easy to lie unmoving in my bunk during the time of "sleep."

The second "day" I went out of the door of my room, not because I had any desire to, but because some small part of my mind which still judged and willed told me that I should learn what I could of this vessel in which I rode. I wandered long gray corridors and saw sights which might almost have overturned my reason had my emotions not been frozen. Not all of the crewmen on that ship were human. Some were like giant lizards without tails, who walked on two feet. Their glittering black eyes had double lids and their face was covered with fine scales which grew larger on what you could see of their bodies. They were clothed, but more lightly clad than the human crewmen, as if they found the rooms too hot. There was a furred creature with three pale blue eyes and a feathered being with a head like an owl's. Some of the crewmen who seemed otherwise human had grayish skin or strange vari-colored eyes.

No one hindered me as I wandered through the corridors and I saw strange sights in some of the rooms that I ventured into. A large room held row after row of crystal boxes, each holding a human infant, dead or frozen in some strange sleep. Another room was like an antechamber to a larger room which was separated from it by a large transparent wall. Beyond the wall seemed to be pale green water in which floated something like a giant flower. But as I stood and gazed eyes opened in the flower and surveyed me with what seemed to be intelligence.

Once I came to a door that seemed to be guarded by a crewman who stood beside it. I looked at him and made a gesture of inquiry. He spoke into a small disc on his wrist, seemed to listen, then touched a circle which opened the door. Inside was a great circular room filled with glittering shapes and lights which marched in slow patterns across panels. Before the panels sat crewmen, some human and some not. Several glanced my way; the feathered creature seeming to turn his head completely around to do so. At one end of the room was a chair like a throne, and behind it a semicircular sweep of carpeted floor. Pacing along this floor in what seemed to be a well-worn path, her hands clasped loosely behind her back, was the captain, Elena Petros. She came to the end of her carpeted area, turned and saw me. She gestured me to come to her and I walked over and stood at the edge of the carpet, somehow reluctant to step onto what seemed a private preserve.

Her face and voice seemed almost normal as she greeted me, but it was all will power and magnificent control; her fine eyes had no sparkle and her body was slack when she did not make it move to her will. "You're very active for a passenger, Citizen Thorn," she said. "Some of them do nothing but stare at the walls. You'll be glad of it when you get planetside; you should be out of freeze in the minimum time. Right now we're busy trying to chart a possible anomaly.

But come back to the bridge after we come out of Q; you'll get a better view of planetfall from here. It won't mean much at the time, but it will be something to remember."

I saluted and left her then, casting an incurious eye on crewmen who stared intently at lighted panels or manipulated curious instruments. Again I exercised, ate and prowled the corridors. Eventually, lights flashed again and a starry sky glowed again on the View in my room. A faint vibration began in the fabric of the ship and after a while one star began to shine more and more brightly. Soon it became a tiny disc, too bright to look at until Pellow touched a circle at the side of the screen and the brilliance faded to a bearable level. "This is a crew cabin," he said. "Cut-off would be automatic on the View in a passenger cabin. Otherwise some passengers would stare at the primary till they damaged their sight."

He stood back from the View, then walked toward it, scanning the stars. Eventually he pointed to a star fainter than many of the others. "That's *a* planet," he said. "Probably Carpathia, because we seem to be heading for it." He pressed another circle beside the view and the stars altered their pattern. The faint star was now a tiny disc and the star which had shone so bright was a white circle near the edge of the View. "Long way out yet," he said. "We won't land until tomorrow. I'd try to sleep if I were you; it will be real sleep now that we're out of Q." I lay down on my bed and after a while began to feel drowsy. For the first time since I had boarded this strange craft I lost consciousness.

I awoke feeling heavy and unrefreshed, cleaned myself up and made my way back to the circular room Elena Petros had called the "bridge." Several panels in the room now showed starry sky with a blue disc in the center. The captain was seated in her thronelike chair and beckoned me to her side. On a great screen which faced her chair I saw starry sky and a blue disc the size of a man's head at the center. It all looked very much as things had looked at the beginning of our voyage and I coldly realized a truth that had, for now, no emotional impact. We had journeyed the heavens, from star to star.

"Let's have extreme magnification on the port city," said Elena Petros, and suddenly the screen before us showed a view from a great height of a sprawling city, even larger than the city I had left to begin this voyage, but on a more human scale with buildings large and small, old and new, jumbled together.

"This is Thorn," said Captain Petros. For a moment I didn't comprehend. Thorn was a little village, huddled below the Castle. Then a familiar outline caught my eye, and my eyes traced the craggy shape of the Hill of Thorn up to the towers and battlements above. There were a few changes, but very few. Standing above the vast alien sprawl of the unfamiliar city was Castle Thorn, the home of my fathers, which I had left, surely, no more than a week ago!

7. Castle Thorn

Elena Petros turned to me and asked with that same controlled appearance of normality, "Are you familiar with the city, Casmir?"

"My ancestors lived there," I said, gesturing at the castle.

She nodded. "Of course, Casmir Thorn; you're named for the city. Your family must have left soon after Rediscovery, though; Carpathia hasn't been in the Commonwealth all that long, if I remember the data fax we got on the planet. Do you have relatives here?"

I shook my head. "I don't know," I said. I wondered in a remote fashion what my emotions would have been if they had not been frozen by the enchanted voyage I had taken. For Thorn to have grown from the village I remembered to this sprawling city must have taken generation upon generation. Had our magical voyage taken centuries? But no, Pellow had said that these star voyages took no real time at all, despite the days that seemed to pass. And Pellow had no reason to lie—or had he? Whom could I trust, whom could I believe in this land of enchanters which seemed to have reached out and engulfed my homeland? The problem was agonizing, but I felt no agony, locked as I was in the frozen emotions which were the price of star voyaging.

We landed in the city as routinely as we had left the city where I had boarded *Argo;* there was another great stretch of the false lawn with the same glowing globes on high poles. There were fewer of the enigmatic structures, and only two of the great discs which must be "starships" like *Argo*. Of course, we felt nothing as the ship landed, but I felt a certain detached admiration for the evident competence and efficiency of Captain Petros and her crew as *Argo* settled her immense bulk on the false greensward as lightly as a leaf falling from a tree.

"Finished with the engines," said Elena Petros. "Open the sally port and prepare to receive planetary officials." She turned to me. "We generally get rid of passengers fairly quickly, Casmir Thorn, but you and your companion are quasi-crew. If you'd like, use your cabin for a while until you get oriented here on Carpathia. The duty officer at the sally port will give you a ship's badge which will get you in and out of the starport and let you use the crew shuttles into the city."

"I thank you, Lady," I said. Was Elena Petros merely being kind, or did she have some hidden motive, I wondered coldly. Perhaps she saw some advantage to be gained from learning more about my reasons for coming to Carpathia. Pellow had told me that the captain of an independent starship like *Argo* had to be a shrewd trader, quick to seize opportunity. Perhaps, too, Elena Petros had some interest in me as a man; there had been a certain spark between us before our emotions had been frozen.

I turned to go, but she stopped me with a gesture. "I don't know what your business is on Carpathia, Casmir Thorn," she said, "but if you're ready to leave before *Argo* lifts, come and see me about a real crew berth. The technical things can be learned—many of them can be autolearned. But the ability to function as well as you did in Q condition is something that's very rare. This flit was just a delivery run. After it, we're outward bound for some trading on our own. There's wealth as well as adventure in the star trade. If that appeals to you, I can always use a good man."

I tried to put some feeling into my voice as I said, "I will remember your words, Captain, and I thank you again." As I left the bridge I considered her offer. I was a man ripped out of his own place and flung into a world which was often incomprehensible. If I could find no way back to my own place, I could certainly do a great deal worse than to join the small, disciplined world of *Argo*. But before I abandoned the world I remembered to try to see what I could make of this new one, I wanted to know how and why I had lost my old world. I had a feeling that Mortifer might know, and Mortifer, according to the "fax" which Benton had given me, was not in this city of Thorn.

If it were not for my frozen emotions, I might have stormed my way into Mortifer's presence and demanded an explanation. But in the cold light of reason, without emotion to influence me, I saw that the better course was to learn everything I could before trying to confront Mortifer. Most of the city was strange to me, but the castle which loomed above the city on its rocky crag was at least outwardly familiar. I decided to make it my first goal.

Benton had given gifts of clothing to me when I left his lodge. During the voyage I had simply pulled on whatever garments came to hand, but now I looked through Benton's gifts and did my best to find garments that would not have looked wildly out of place at my father's court. At the sally port I was given a little circular patch of black which seemed to have a star gleaming in its center. "Most of us wear them over our C and C chip," said the duty officer. "Marks us as starcrew and it's no business of the planetaries how much credit we have, since we pay in ecus anyway. Captain said to treat you as crew, so I'll give you the same advice as I'd give a new crewman. Stay in the port area until you come out of freeze; planetaries are often scared of starcrew or hostile to them. They don't understand freeze and they have strange ideas about it. If you're anxious to get out of freeze as quickly as possible, don't fool around with the so-called emotional therapists; go to a blackout."

At my look of incomprehension, he explained, "They're plays, short and pretty melodramatic. But somehow all that stage emotion seems to unfreeze your own emotions. See a good blackout and get a good night's sleep and by tomorrow morning you may begin to feel human. If not, repeat the treatment. We were two days on GE drive that's two days out of Q. Cutting it a little fine, but you kept active in Q and that helps."

I hesitated, then decided to take his advice. Much as I grudged the time, I realized that a man in emotional freeze was conspicuous and I did not want to be conspicuous when I set out to find what I could about Mortifer and about what had happened to me.

There was certainly nothing recognizable and almost nothing Carpathian about the area around the starport. The men and women who filled the taverns and wandered the streets in various stages of emotional freeze were the same strange mixture of faces as I had encountered aboard *Argo*, along with others even stranger; lithe, brown creatures who seemed to slither rather than walk, and exotically plumed beings who almost seemed to float along.

It was easy enough to find a blackout; there were several theaters near the starport gates. The first surprise was that the play featured both humans and the sealed lizard-like creatures I had learned to call Szilara. There were four players, a male and female Szilar, a man and a woman.

The plot, looking back on it, was thin enough stuff; a tale of danger and hairsbreadth escapes with the Szilara as villains, the woman as victim and the man as rescuing hero. But it was well written and well acted. At first it seemed merely interesting, then it became absorbing. At a tense moment in the plot I found myself gripping the arms of my seat and realized that my emotions were returning. By the end of the play I was joining in the catcalls which greeted the appearance of the villains and shouting myself hoarse to cheer on the hero.

The play ended abruptly with the lights turned out at a high point of tension; the "blackout" from which the plays took their name. As the lights went on again and the audience filed out, I exchanged sheepish smiles with other men and women whose badges proclaimed them as starcrew. We felt foolish, but we felt human again.

It was late and I headed for the starport gates, planning to get some proper rest and head for the castle in the morning. A small man in brown caught my attention with a courteous gesture as I strolled away from the theater and I paused to see what he wanted of me. On closer inspection there was something rather unpleasant about his smooth manner and foppish appearance, and I regretted not having ignored him. He came to my side and spoke in a low rapid voice, not looking at my face; "The honorable startrader may wish to complete his emotional recovery by sampling our wares," he said, "the finest gynas, perfect simulacra of the most beautiful women in the Commonwealth, programmed for your pleasure . . ."

I did not completely understand what he was offering, but I understood well enough to be disgusted. "Be off with you!" I said and raised my hand as if to cuff him. He cringed and slid off into the shadows.

"Good for you, flitter," said a woman's voice behind me. I turned to see a richly dressed woman of considerable beauty, with a hardness to her voice and features that let me guess her profession. "Too many flitters are spending their credit on those mechanical dolls. Afraid of a real woman, most of them. If you're not, I'll give you a special rate for sending that puppet pimp about his business."

I gave her a grin. "Not tonight, my pretty one. But good hunting," I said. She gave a little trill of laughter, raised a hand in salute and strolled languidly off, her eyes searching the faces of the men who were emerging from the theater.

Back aboard *Argo* I found Pellow lying on his bunk and told him of my adventures. He nodded dully, still wrapped in emotional freeze. "Yes, blackouts will do the job all right, but I don't want out of freeze until I leave this ship," he said. "It will be bad enough knowing I can't flit again except as a passenger without living in crew quarters and seeing starflitters about me every day. I'll look for lodgings in the city tomorrow, I think. What about you?"

I hesitated. "I may know more after tomorrow. Don't leave *Argo* for good without leaving me word of where I can find you." He nodded listlessly and was stretching out again as I asked, "These gynas the man spoke of, what are they? The bawdy called them dolls, and puppets . . ."

Pellow shrugged. "That's what they are, mechanicals just like andros. Technically I suppose they'd have to expose the blue dome under their wigs if they ever went out of doors. But you'll never find them outside a bawdy house. Physically they're a perfect replica of a woman but their programming is pretty limited; they're made for only one thing. The ones that are replicas of famous actresses and other well known women are kept in pretty tight seclusion; their owners would be in big trouble if the duplication could be proved. You hear stories of women who've been copied without their permission hiring wilders to break up a bawdy house and destroy the gynas. On the other hand, you hear stories of 3V stars who let themselves be duplicated for a share of the profits."

I groped for a way to put the question I wanted to ask without exposing my ignorance. "The andros—I've seen none of them here so far."

Pellow shook his head. "No, I wouldn't expect to see any here. They can't flit, the effect of Q on them are too unpredictable. A general-purpose andro like we were pretending to be costs a small fortune to build; more than most cits make in five years. It's not worthwhile making them on a backwater planet like this; there are humans to do even the most menial jobs. Gynas are another matter; you can always peddle exotic sex, especially near a starport."

I fell into my bunk, my head whirling. The "andros," then, were some sort of doll or puppet, moved by enchanters' arts. No wonder they gaped and stared in poor imitation of humanity. But what about the serfs I remembered, surely they were natural men, born and not built by magical arts. But except for their shocks of unkempt hair . . . Suddenly I had a sort of double image; serfs as I had remembered them up to now and then a different set of images: serfs grinning, laughing, drinking; buxom serf women smiling at me and shock-headed children tumbling on the cottage floors. My heart pounded and I broke out in a sweat. Up to now I had not doubted my memories. I had reckoned myself a sane man in a mad world of enchantment. What if it was I that was mad . . . ?

I made myself breathe deeply and relax. Whatever had been done to me, some things I could hold to. I knew enough of hunting to win Benton's respect. I could handle myself well enough in this strange world to make Elena Petros offer me a berth on *Argo*. Whatever I learned about myself I was my own man and could hold my own in this or any other world. And surely my memories of Castle Thorn and my life there could not all be false. I knew that castle as well as I knew my own hands—or did I? Tomorrow would tell. I made myself sleep.

The next day it took an effort to keep my voice steady as I asked the guard at the starport gate about transportation to the castle. He shrugged. "Oh yes, you can get there all right, they run tours. But not many flitters care to go. Tell you what, go over to the passenger gate round the fence there; cut across the field. There are probably regular tours leaving from there for visitors with time to kill here. Some of the tours are free; the city merchants run them to attract business. I'd take off your crew badge and hope they take you for a wealthy cit."

I thanked the man and cut across the false grass to the gate he had indicated. A more grandly dressed gatekeeper looked at me oddly, then told me to wait. Presently he returned with another man. "The regular tour is gone, citizen, but Jelleck here will give you a lift to the castle gate and find a tour you can join." I thanked him and accompanied the other man to a moving platform smaller and faster than the one I had ridden with the andros the day I first met Pellow. I settled in a seat beside the man named Jelleck and was whisked through crowded streets toward the castle. Nothing I saw looked familiar until we came to the castle gates. Where I remembered a moat there was a broad paved area, but the gates themselves and the walls above were heart-stoppingly familiar.

The man named Jelleck looked around him. "If you'll wait here, citizen, I'll find a guide for you," he said, and entered the castle through a small postern gate that I did not remember. I climbed off the platform and stretched. Another unfamiliar object near the gates was a statue standing immediately before the gates, a man in armor with an unfurled flag in one hand and a bared sword in the other. I strolled casually over to look at it and was suddenly standing there staring, unable to move. Dimly I heard a child's voice behind me, "Mama, look! The man standing there looks just like the statute of King Casmir the Protector!"

8. The Hall of Kings

I heard a chuckle at my side and turned to see a young man with a studious look about him, clothed in a shabby robe that looked somewhat like a monk's habit. "The child's right, ser," he said. "You're the spitting image of the Blessed King. You must have Jagellon blood all right, though by your clothing you're from off-planet. Would you like a guide, ser? I'm a poor student and I promise you that your fee will all be spent on students' necessaries—books and wine."

I laughed, liking the look of the young man, and flipped him one of the golden discs from my pouch; since one had bought me admittance to the blackout I reckoned it a fair fee for a guide. His face grew grave and with an obvious struggle he made as if to hand it back to me. "This is far too much for a guide, ser," he said. "And I can't give you exchange."

I pushed his hand away. "Keep it for your studies then, ser scholar," I said, "and enough wine not to interfere with the studying."

He laughed at that, but his eyes were bright as he carefully stowed the disc in his clothing. "This will buy me things from off-planet that will save me much time in my studies," he said awkwardly. "I thank you, ser, and I'm at your disposal for as long as you like. Come round to the Little Gate, going through the gift shop yonder spoils the castle for anyone with taste. Do you know any Carpathian history, ser, or should I start at the beginning?"

"Treat me like a child at his first lessons," I said.

He chuckled again and fell into a lecturing tone as we

walked along the paved area with the castle walls soaring above us. "Well, ser, Carpathia was colonized just before the Wars of Unity when, of course, the remoter colonies were soon cut off. A Szilar raider torched the techno complex, which they hadn't had time to decentralize, and the planet slid right back to the feudal age in a few generations. The colonists had to go back to the most primitive subsistence farming and the starcrew who were stranded here when their ship was torched became a feudal aristocracy. The captain of the ship was a man named Casmir Jagellon who had a hobby of reading ancient history from Home. He formed his crew into an order of knighthood and got about the long task of building up civilization again . . ."

"To restore the Golden Days . . ." I said softly. It was a phrase from my knightly oath.

The young scholar shot me a startled glance. "But if you know the oath of the Knights of Thorn . . ." he began.

I shook my head, "Never mind, go on as you began," I said. "A child at his first lessons."

He shrugged and went on. "Well, ser, Casmir Jagellon became King Casmir the First and built the first castle here on Castle Crag. Some colonists revolted and went off to found their own societies. But most of those reverted to barbarism. Actually we know more about this early history than we do about the later history of Carpathia because for a while some sophisticated recording devices survived which could make record chips. When those broke down or wore out records were kept only with pen and ink on reed paper, and not all of these records survived. There was a Dark Age, a period from which more legends and myth than real history survive. For instance, if you look at the shield of King Casmir the Protector on the statue outside you'll see a winged fire-breathing lizard, a firedrake. Most scholars now say they're only legends, influenced by old stories from Home like the Bilbo-saga. Some scholars think they really existed, but they're in the minority."

"Why does . . . King Casmir . . . have one on his shield?" I asked.

He chuckled. "Oh, the usual thing, he killed a firedrake and rescued a princess."

"Was her name Delora?" I asked, trying to keep my voice calm.

The young scholar shook his head. "Oh no, one of the Hedwigas, I think. Delora isn't a Carpathian name, even, and I'm sure it doesn't come into any of the legends."

A day or so ago I would have backed my own memory against a scholar's knowledge of legends but with my new uncertainty his words gave me a sharp stab of uneasiness. "How about Mortifer?" I said.

He laughed. "Oh yes, he comes into that legend as a cross between the wicked enchanter and the usurping regent. King Casmir eventually banished him, I think. But there are a lot of Mortifers in Carpathian history, some heroes, and some villains. Mortifer is one of the old Carpathian family names, probably descended from one of the original starcrew, though that name doesn't appear on the log as we have it. Ah, here's the Little Gate."

We entered a small but richly decorated gate; again its position but not its style matched my memories. As I expected, we stood within the courtyard of the castle with the Great Tower soaring above us. Built into the wall near us was a small church; the scholar led me into its nave and left me to look at the great altar and the carved and gilded statues while he crossed himself and knelt briefly to pray. I stood looking about me, while more suppressed memories flitted through my mind; Mass at the high altar with the flash of swords and sound of trumpets at the Elevation, catechism lessons from an old priest who had been my tutor before Mortifer. How could I have forgotten?

The scholar did not speak until we were out of the church; then he said quietly, "That chapel is still the Cathedral of Thorn and for the Carpathians who keep the Old Faith, the holiest place on Carpathia. The First Chaplain is buried there and Holy Queen Hedwig. Not the kings, though, they're all buried in the Hall of Kings on the other side of the castle. There was quite a furor a few years ago when some scientists from the Royal Academy got permission to examine some of the bodies for archeological purposes. Carpathia isn't a monarchy anymore, of course, but the Old Carpathia Party talked about desecration of our history."

"The king who stands before the castle . . ." I said slowly.

He nodded. "Your look-alike? He was Casmir the Tenth. He united all the little kingdoms and really started Carpathia on the road to civilization. You couldn't be descended from him; he was quite a devout man by all accounts and faithful to the princess he rescued. Some of his descendants were a bit more—er—prolific and no doubt your family . . . Well, the direct line died out before Rediscovery and if there had been a legitimate cadet branch . . ."

He was growing more embarrassed as he tangled himself in explanations. "I take your point," I said. "How is Carpathia ruled now?"

The scholar looked troubled. "Theoretically it's a Direct Democracy," he said, "but the old families interfere a lot. The present Mortifer doesn't hold political office, he's an Academician, but according to the Old Carpathia Party he has a lot more influence than he should have on government decisions. Right now he's in some sort of trouble at Home and the government is resisting attempts to extradite or even question him. Well, you're not interested in Carpathian politics. Would you like to see the Great Tower or . . ."

"The Hall of Kings, I think," I told him. "What sort of thing does this Mortifer do? Does he live here in Thorn?"

"Oh yes," said the young man. "He has a suite of rooms at the Royal Academy which a lot of scholars think should be put to use as research space; another example of his influence. They must be some of the best rooms in the city way up at the top of the building like that. Here, let's go up the guards' stair and along the battlements. You can see the Academy over on Hedwiga's Hill across the valley." As I followed the young scholar up the well worn familiar steps I reflected that my golden circle had been well spent. The young man was so eager to please me that I had only to express interest in a subject to be flooded with all of the information the young man had.

"There's Hedwiga's Hill, with the Institute on top," said my companion as we reached the battlements. As I had half expected, "Hedwiga's Hill" was the Mount of Sacrifice. There looked to be a small chapel of some sort on the ledge where I remembered fighting the firedrake, and the top of the hill had been carved and quarried so that the whole top of the hill was a great building. It was built of the gray local stone, but had no battlements or towers; it looked more like a monastery than a castle, but somehow it echoed the look of the castle whose walls we stood on. Some master builder had taken care to see that the two buildings which dominated the town below should not jar with each other.

The town itself was a fairer sight, looked at from this more human height, than it had been from *Argo*. I could see the glint of fountains in the squares and the green of parks scattered here and there among the streets. Around the castle were the old winding streets that I remembered, but farther away the streets went in broader curves that followed lines of the country. The rigid geometry of the city of enchanters where I had boarded Argo was happily absent. I began to feel a sense of belonging here, a sense of possession, and with it a sense of responsibility. "A beautiful city," I said to the scholar.

He nodded, slowly looking out over the city. "Yes," he said quietly. "I want to travel through the Commonwealth; there's so much to see, to learn. But always I'll want to come back to Thorn, to meditate on what I've learned. I don't know whether I'll ever be elected to the Academy over there, but there are humbler places where perhaps more real scholarship goes on . . ."

Just then I heard footsteps on the stairs we had come up, and turned to see the man Jelleck, who had brought me to the castle from the starport. He was followed by a burly man who eyed me with a curiously appraising look. "I've found you a guide, ser," said Jelleck, gesturing to the man beside him.

"Thanks for that," I told him, "but I have found my own guide." If there had been some small coins in my pouch, I might have tossed him one; but if a golden "ecu" was too much for a guide, it was too much for the smaller service he had rendered, and my supply of the little circlets was limited.

My young scholar-guide cut in, "You're not one of the regular guides," he told the burly man. "Where's your medallion? The Castle guides barely tolerate us scholars guiding people here; you can get into serious trouble doing guide's work without authorization."

Jelleck opened his mouth but the other man took his arm in what looked like no gentle grip. "We had a guide waiting for you below," said the burly man glibly. "But if the citizen here has no need of him, we'll dismiss him. Come on, Jelleck." He hustled Jelleck back down the stairs.

The scholar grinned at me. "The tough had better sense than the tout," he said. "Some unauthorized guiding does go on, of course, because you can't be sure that one person showing another the castle isn't just a citizen showing a country cousin the sights of Thorn. But if anyone is caught taking a fee, the official guides will take it to court. That muscleman looked the type who might try to bully an extra fee out of a timid tourist; he'll get nailed for Uncivil behavior someday, if that's his game. Not that he'd get far with you, ser."

I smiled at that, but I realized now what the burly man's look of appraisal had been; the look of one fighting man sizing up another. A faint chill of uneasiness came over me. Even if Jelleck was a rogue and had some dishonest ploy in mind, was he not risking a great deal, since I knew his name and he was known to the gateman at the starport? The sense of being pursued, which had faded with my other emotions on *Argo*, came back in full force. I looked around me as the scholar talked of kings and battles, trying to think of what I could do if I were attacked here. How many memories of this castle could I trust, how much would this strangely altered Castle Thorn fight on my side?

The Hall of Kings was new to me; a strongly built place half hall and half chapel perched on a crag at one side of the castle and connected to the battlements by a high-flung bridge of wood. I hesitated before setting foot on the bridge; the place was a cul de sac. Still, not many could come at me at once over that bridge; the passage could be defended fairly easily by a determined man.

As if echoing my thought the young scholar said, "Casmir the Fourteenth made a stand here when his enemies seized the Castle by treachery. He burned the bridge behind him and held out until loyal troops relieved him. Later renovaters have wanted to rebuild the bridge in stone but the traditionalists have always objected, and so the bridge is wooden just as in the days it was burned. Of course, the timbers have been renewed, but it still makes some visitors from high-tech worlds nervous; they don't really trust natural materials like wood."

The bridge was sturdy enough, and the interior of the hall which we entered through massive wooden doors had a dignified simplicity. There was a central aisle lit by clerstory windows above, and off of this aisle was a series of alcoves like small side chapels in a great church. Some of these contained obvious mausoleums, others held statuary groups or plaques. A shield hung above the entrance to each alcove and a flagstaff projected above each shield. The flags on the staffs were tattered and faded, but you could see the Crown and Sword design on each; they had been the personal standards of the dead kings.

I walked softly down the aisle until I came to an alcove below a familiar shield. The alcove contained nothing but a massive rectangular slab of dark stone. Plunged into the stone slab as if driven there by a mighty force was a sword I recognized. I stood there gazing somberly at it, wondering if

I were a ghost or a living man, whether I stood before this dark slab or lay beneath it.

A sharp gasp from the young scholar aroused me from my reverie. Following his gaze I saw the burly man who had accosted us along with Jelleck, striding across the bridge. He was followed by three men even bigger and brawnier and all of them looked grim and purposeful. Suddenly the gatekeeper's odd looks at me and his delays, Jelleck's odd eagerness to help me into the city and the burly man's appraising glance came together into a sinister pattern. I had been sniffed out by the faceless enemies who pursued me and skillfully herded into this trap, a trap that was about to close on me!

9. Face to Face

My next move was half instinctive, half desperation. I reached for the hilt of the sword on the tomb and pulled. It came as easily into my hand as if it had been in a greased sheath. Above my head a great bell tolled once; perhaps an alarm set off by my impulsive action. But I had no time to think of that; I ran sword in hand for the door, to meet my attackers on the bridge where they could surround me. I took a grim delight in their faces as I burst out of the door, sword at the ready. The first man fumbled at his belt, but before he could draw any weapon I had dealt him a stunning blow on the side of his head with the flat of my sword. He crumpled to the floor of the bridge and I leaped over his body to dash the pommel of the sword into the face of the next man following. He staggered back into the arms of the next man and two quick swipes with the flat of the sword stunned them both. The last man was a little out of reach, but I feinted a thrust at him to keep him off balance. His nerve broke and he turned and ran.

I wheeled to see if any of the others were recovering, but the young scholar was standing over them with what looked like a heavy candlestick, snatched perhaps from some altar in the Hall of Kings. We exchanged grins and he started to speak, but suddenly there was a curious sound, half howl, half whistle, from the air above us. I looked up to see a circular platform swooping down upon us. On it stood a woman in dark blue garments with a stylized shield covering her chest and a close-fitting helmet on her head. "Oh lord, a monitor,'' said the scholar. ''If these men deny that they meant to attack us . . .''

I stepped close to him and with an odd reluctance pressed the sword hilt into his hand. ''Keep this under your robe and walk slowly into the Hall,'' I said in a low voice. ''Restore the sword to where it came from while I parley with this . . . monitor.'' If the woman approaching us was a keeper of the law I had no wish to use a sword on her, and if I had no weapon in my hand I could play the injured innocent better. The scholar grinned again and slipped unobtrusively back to the door of the Hall as the woman maneuvered her flying platform to land on the wide space on the battlements where the bridge to the Hall of Kings began.

As soon as her platform touched ground the ''monitor'' leaped lightly off of it and came toward me, a stubby instrument of familiar aspect held in one hand, the dark lens pointing at my chest.

''What's going on?'' she asked in a voice that was musical yet filled with authority.

I had decided on a story that kept fairly close to the truth. ''This man offered himself as a guide; when I refused he grew angry. When he came at me with three companions I thought it best to strike first.''

She lifted an elegantly arched eyebrow, stepped past me without taking her eyes from me or ceasing to train her weapon on me and turned over one of my assailants with a booted foot. ''Their faces make good witnesses to your story,'' she drawled. ''This one's a known tough and Wilder. If you'd come to my prowler, citizen, I'd like a statement from you.''

At her gesture I preceded her to the platform, which was surmounted by a stubby, waist-high column which held blinking lights and cryptic levers. ''Step on the black area, please,'' she said and I did so. She stepped on the platform opposite me and put a hand on the column. Suddenly we were in the air and I clutched frantically for a hand-hold which protruded from the column. ''I'll return you to Castle Thorn after your statement,'' she said calmly. I risked a glance below to see houses spread below us like a pampered child's model city. When a bird flew *under* us I turned my gaze to the sky. The woman smiled slightly. "You can't fall off," she said. "The gravity effect keeps you on." I tried to look a great deal calmer than I felt, but I probably did not deceive her.

My stomach protested as we swooped down again to land. I looked around; we were on the roof of a building which towered high over the city; I could see Castle Thorn on its crag across the valley filled with houses. Suddenly an alarm bell tolled in my mind. This must be the building on "Hedwiga's Hill," the Academy as they called it. Below me, perhaps just under my feet were the apartments of Mortifer!

I must have stiffened because the woman took a step back and trained her weapon on me. "I see you've guessed something," she said. "You have two choices now, walk or be carried. It will be easier for both of us if you walk." I shrugged and followed her directions to stand on a marked area of the roof. She spoke into a small disc she took from her belt and the whole area flashed white and vanished; we sank slowly into the room below, a featureless antechamber. A door flashed into being on one wall and I was ushered into a richly furnished room. Seated on a thronelike chair was the man I had come so far to see, Mortifer the Enchanter. I was meeting him on his own terms, but at least we were face to face at last.

There was no other chair in the room but there was a massive table not far from him; I strolled over to it and sat on its edge. Crossing my legs I waited for Mortifer to break the silence. He had to turn his head a little to see me and his lips tightened with an annoyance he could not quite hide from me.

The woman's voice came from behind me. "He laid out three of the toughs and the other took to his heels. Lucky I was there in reserve, Councillor."

Mortifer's voice was dry as he said, "You did your job, they did not. It is noted." He was always a bad leader, grudging of his praise and cruel in his reprimands.

I turned my head to look at the woman and gave her a smile. "You were quick and clever," I said. "Well played." She was so startled that she returned my smile for a moment until Mortifer's growl took the smile and the color from her face and sent her scurrying out of the room.

I turned to Mortifer. "You're better served than you deserve," I said, "as always."

He glowered, but did not rise to the bait. "You would have stood where you are standing long before this," he said, "if you had not been a stubborn maker of trouble."

"As always?" I asked blandly and his control snapped.

"Always!" he sneered in icy rage. "You are a creature of a moment; I grew you in my tanks not two years ago. What you think you remember I put into your head, except for those two years. During that time you were a puppet in a toy theater of my devising. For a while it looked as if I might learn a little from you, but interfering fools spoiled that. You're a bit of apparatus for a botched experiment; it's time to throw you on the trash pile before you do more damage."

It was something I had half feared, ever since I had heard the story of Justinian Droste's case against Mortifer and then soon after the story of young Benton's boars. Yet there was some comfort in that, if I understood it rightly. "Grown, perhaps," I said, "but from what? Did you desecrate a dead king's body for the flesh from which you grew me, Mortifer of the *Royal* Academy? And if you did, can I not say that I **am** Casmir's flesh and Casmir's bone? Can't I say, even that I **am** Casmir?"

His eyes lit up with a dark glee as he replied. "Your prototype was always enamored with hair-splitting and useless metaphysics. It seems that I didn't manage to suppress that in you. Well, riddle me this, metaphysician. If growing you from Casmir's tissue samples makes you Casmir, then what about the other one I grew from those samples? If you are identical with Casmir, so is he. But things equal to the same thing are equal to each other, aren't they? So you two must be the same. But you're not; for one thing you're here and the other one is—elsewhere. So neither of you can be Casmir."

It was a shock, but it was also a triumph, for I felt sure that it had been no part of his plan to tell me of this other Casmir. Trying to keep an appearance of calm and keep pressure on Mortifer, I shrugged and drew myself up to sit tailor fashion on the table. "It doesn't follow, Mortifer; you were always weak at logic," I said mockingly. "All you've proved is that both of us can't be the original Casmir, not that one of us can't."

Weak at logic or not Mortifer had a passion for argument; I had often lured him into disputes when his lessons bored me. He leaned forward, clutching the arms of his chair, his face dark with anger. "Nonsense," he said venomously. "There's nothing to choose between you; cultured from the same sample, put in identical artificial environments, subjected to the same stimuli. That was the point of the whole thing; to show, to prove that you'd act identically, that humans are as much machines as andros are, that free will is a philosopher's dream!"

"And did you prove it?" I said mockingly, probing at the weakness I sensed behind his bluster.

His refusal to answer was itself an answer. He rose to his feet, his eyes blazing. "The experiment was botched, spoiled," he cried, "and now its time to throw away the mess that's left."

I tensed, but my feet were not quite set—if I could only buy a moment's time . . . Then a faint musical note sounded from the back of Mortifer's chair and a woman's voice said, "Councillor, there's a mob coming up the Hill toward the institute."

Mortifer half turned toward the chair back and said impatiently, "A mob? What has that to do with me? How dare you interrupt . . ."

The voice, which I was sure was that of the woman who had brought me here said, "Ser, they're led by a man in a scholar's robe; I think the same fellow I saw just before I landed at the Castle, talking to the man who is in there with you. And they're shouting something . . . something very odd. Something about 'Casmir's come again.' "

There was a moment's silence and I could hear Mortifer grinding his teeth, a nasty habit of his when in a rage. "Prepare the disposal chamber," he said after a moment. "They'll find no Casmir here."

"But ser," the voice came, "this man is . . . you said he was little more than an andro, but . . ." I blessed the impulse that had made me praise the woman and make some sort of human contact with her. It was a good moment to improve on, that contact.

"I am a citizen of the Commonwealth," I said, baring my wrist with its green circle, hoping that the woman could see into the chamber by some spyhole. "Have you no laws against killing a citizen? Is there no punishment for that, even for Mortifer's servants? For the killer at least, even if he escapes?" My feet were nearly set now; it was hellishly uncomfortable but they were side by side under my buttocks, with enough contact with the table to give me some leverage. I slouched to give my arms as much flex as possible; my hands were flat on the table.

"I'll torch you myself," screamed Mortifer, beginning to draw something from his garments, "and that insubordinate bitch," I launched myself straight into his face, with every ounce of my strength, bringing my arms up after I leaped so that my clenched fists on either side of my head made my head and arms the head of a human battering ram.

My leap was not quite as strong as I had hoped; I struck him in the chest and not in the face. He was protected in some way, it was like hitting an image of stone but my weight and momentum could not completely be nullified by his defenses; I heard his breath whoosh out and his chair went over with a resounding crash, sending us both to the floor. I grabbed him by the arms and rolled toward the heavy table I had been sitting on. He would hardly have received me alone without guardsmen to hand but if I could get that table between me and the door and keep hold of Mortifer perhaps I could make him my hostage.

Now we were under the table. I lay with all my weight on Mortifer and kicked the table top from underneath. It toppled, and I had my barricade. Suddenly I felt Mortifer's arms move in my hands and something hard thrust into my belly. "Let go," Mortifer grated, "or I'll torch your guts out." If he could have done it without risk to himself, my racing brain told me, he would have done it, not threatened; I made as if to obey, relaxing my hold on his arms, then as he thrust me away from him, I dropped my hands to capture his and jerked suddenly upwards. Over his head, his weapon would be useless, and I could pin him again.

Suddenly there was a blinding flash; my eyes were dazzled and my face burned. I could smell my own burned hair and for a moment all I could do was hold on frantically. But then there was no strength to Mortifer's limbs, no resistance, and I raised myself to hands and knees, peering down at the ruined body below me. There was an acrid smell, but it was not the smell of burned flesh. Liquid flowed sluggishly, but it was dark, not red. I looked down, and as the dazzle cleared from my vision I saw below me the wreck of Mortifer's form. The false flesh curled back like burned parchment and beneath it was the glint of half molten metal, uncounted tiny threads of varied colors, enigmatic crystals. Mortifer, the enchanter, was a magical puppet, not human flesh and blood! Then my dazzled senses failed, my overstrained muscles relaxed and I fell to the floor, half conscous of a rending sound behind me, as the floor seemed to shake, then strike me in the face with a mighty blow.

Part II

10. Under the Hills

Firedrake slayer; a good name to die with if one must die. As the mighty monster slipped off the edge I thrust my left hand into a rent in the wing I had made with my dirk, and plunged the dirk itself into the base of the wing, using it again as an anchor. My feet scrabbled, but could find no purchase; I hung by my hands alone as we left the ledge, and the frantic beating of the blinded beast's other wing tossed us in mad spirals. Down, down, down, nearer to death on the crags below. I was hanging below the beast, it would land on me and crush me.

A branch whipped my cheek and I suddenly smelled evergreen sap. With the greatest effort of will of my life I made my hands release their hold and I fell through the air. Branches cracked, my fall slowed, and for a second I dared to hope. Then my leg hit something solid and snapped as the branches had snapped. There was a terrible pain and I lost consciousness.

There were fevered dreams afterward that seemed to last for centuries. But one day I awoke to brightness in my eyes and the smell of bread baking somewhere. A serf's dull eyes were regarding me from a face that seemed to float above me. Then as I tried to move the face vanished and I nearly lost consciousness again in the pain from my leg and ribs and head. The room swam around me, then came into focus again; my own room at Castle Thorn. The sword of my fathers was back in its rack on the wall, a newly painted shield beside it. The arms were my own, the sword and crown, but without the "file," the "difference" which marked me as the oldest son of the king. That shield should be borne by my father, not by me. I was staring dully at the shield, my mind refusing to work, when Stanislaus, the court physician, bustled into the room, his face beaming.

"Hail, firedrake slayer!" he said. "Hail, Casmir, protector of the kingdom! Rest now and heal. All is well." I must have made some feeble gesture toward the shield, because his face became grave. "Your father's heart could not hold the sorrow of your peril and the joy of your victory without bursting," he said solemnly. "Casmir the Ninth is dead. Long live King Casmir, Tenth of the Line!" That was too much and I lapsed into unconsciousness again.

After that were long lazy days and nights with less pain and fewer nightmares. Delora came to me once or twice, suitably chaperoned and laid a cool hand on my brow. Her skin was reddened and her eyebrows and lashes scorched away, but she was lovely as ever. Her thanks were flowery, but had little real warmth behind them and a dull irritation stirred under my lethargy. She was lovely but was there a real woman behind that beautiful facade? I remembered . . . what did I remember? Laughing faces, tender looks . . . Were they real memories, or fantasies? I slept again.

Little triumphs marked my days; cutting my own meat, being supported, none too gently, by two serfs as I got out of bed to use the garderobe. There was a day when I knew that I had my life back, if not all my strength; I was a man who had been broken and was weak, no longer a broken man. It was on that day my old life ended.

I was lying in my bed in a sort of restful doze, postponing the moment that I would have to take up the reins of power. Mortifer was away and that gave me time to drift and heal. As soon as he returned there would be a test of wills, one I meant to win. My father's age and weakness—yes weakness, I could call it by its name now—no longer put me in Mortifer's power. I was no longer his pupil and would never be his puppet. I was determined to show him that. If only the

Falling Sickness did not betray me, as it had done before in confrontations with Mortifer . . .

Suddenly I realized that the small noises of the everyday functioning of the castle had ceased. I looked over at the serf who stood by the door ready to summon help or run errands. He was unnaturally still and as I gazed at him I realized that he was not breathing, not even blinking. The hair rose on the back of my neck and my skin tingled. Enchantment! Mortifer must be back, and this must be his way of attack, sudden, swift and silent. Was I, too, paralyzed? No, I felt as fit and able as ever. As blood coursed in my body in response to the challenge I felt fitter than I had since my fight with the firedrake. I leaped to my feet, and ripped my sword and shield from the wall. I thrust my feet into the soft boots beside the bed and tiptoed to the door.

It opened silently; the hinges had been well-oiled, not to disturb a wounded man's sleep. In the corridor a serf and a mirror courtier stood frozen like statues. I crept softly past them, my ears straining for any sound. There! That could only be the gates of the Great Hall being opened; I would know that creak and groan anywhere. A small stair not far along this corridor would bring me out onto the dais; it was a way for the royal family to slip away from a feast that went on too long. Should I take a more indirect way? No! The King of Carpathia should face his enemies boldly, not creep like a rat in his own hold!

They were standing in the center of the Great Hall, a little knot of men in strange garments. Their leader was not Mortifer, but a man I had never seen before in strange close-fitting garments of green so dark it was almost black in some lights. Behind him was a man in brown with a strange object, which gleamed and sparkled . . . in his hands? No, floating in the air before him! Enchantments!

They had not seen me yet; they were gaping around the Hall. I stepped suddenly out onto the dais, letting my sword touch my shield to make a small ringing sound. Every eye turned to me, but no one made a hostile move. The green-clad leader looked at me impassively, but the man in brown gasped, "The same man—the same in every detail!"

The leader said in a steady voice, "That was what we might have expected, given what else we know." He turned his gray eyes to me and said, "I am Justinian Droste. You are . . . Casmir?"

I nodded, trying to keep my face impassive. "Casmir, King of Carpathia, tenth of the Line. And you, I suppose, are creatures of Mortifer's?"

The man named Justinian Droste gave a short laugh and said with apparent sincerity, "We're no friends to Mortifer, King Casmir. In fact, we're here to help you against Mortifer, if you'll let us. Help you in ways you can hardly guess at yet."

I lifted a skeptical eyebrow at them. "And what do you want in return for your—help?" All the same my blood was pounding in excitement. Mortifer was powerful and wily; despite all my royal power and authority I had half-feared the issue of any struggle between us. But with a rival gang of enchanters on my side, perhaps I could break Mortifer, break him and banish him as I had longed to do ever since he had wormed his way into my father's confidence.

Droste looked into my eyes and said softly, "We want to bring Mortifer down. Just that. Will you help us?"

I held his eyes for a long moment and then nodded slowly. "If I can do it without prejudice to my people and my kingdom, I will."

Justinian Droste sighed. "Your people and your kingdom, yes. I'm afraid that's the first shock I have for you. But after the mistakes we made last time I'm determined to tell you everything. Perhaps it's easier to show you than to tell you, though." He walked over to the side of the hall; one of the castle serfs was frozen there where he had been wiping a table. Droste took a small globe from a pouch at his waist and pressed it, making a fine mist issue from a small orifice at one side of the globe. Droste directed the spray at his own hand and rubbed it lightly into the wrist. "This stuff is harmless," he said, "just a solvent for a common adhesive. Notice that it does nothing to the hair on the back of my hand."

He stepped over to the serf, lifted the fellow's shock of hair and sprayed under it. Then he pulled gently and the whole head of hair came off in his hand. Under it was a dome of gleaming metallic blue, like a skullcap, coming almost to the serf's eyebrows. Justinian Droste stepped back and nodded to the man in brown who touched the blue dome with a small glittering object, then put both of his hands on the dome and gave it a sharp twist. The whole top of the serf's head came off in his hands and he laid it on the table the serf had been wiping. The thing was like a mushroom; the "stem" had been inside the lower part of the serf's head.

"A control unit," said Droste. "This is a fairly standard low-level general purpose android, generally called an 'andro.' All of the servitors in this place are of the same type; they haven't even bothered to give them false foreheads under that mop of hair. I take it that you've been conditioned not to pay much attention to servitors, so they didn't take much trouble with them." He turned to the man in brown. "Andres, give me the stat of the plot of the other place." He studied a sheet of what looked like parchment or stiff cloth for a moment then said formally, "Follow me, please, King Casmir."

"Wait," I said. "This—thing—is not flesh and blood? It is a . . . puppet, moved by magical arts?" Droste nodded, his face grave. I laid my shield on the table and gripped my sword. Trying to think of what remained of the serf as no more than a lay figure for practice, I swung the sword over my head and dealt the thing a mighty blow. What was left of the head and one shoulder and arm bounced to the floor. There was no blood and no bone, only the gleam of metal, the glitter of some sort of crystal, and a tangle of multicolored threads and tubes. "Yes," I said, dully, "yes, the thing is—what you said."

"By the Mercy," said the man in brown, whom Droste had called Andres. "If you went on 3V with that act, you'd make a fortune." Droste gave him a sharp look and he fell silent, following Droste and myself as we headed for the main staircase out of the Hall. I stole a glance at the glittering object he pushed along with him; without a doubt it did float in the air.

Droste led me to an ornamental door and turned. "What is behind this door, King Casmir?" he asked. "Have you ever been inside it?"

I shook my head. "It is the Ladies' Suite," I said, "the Solar, the bedchambers of the unmarried court ladies, sewing rooms and the like. As a bachelor knight it is all forbidden territory to me."

Droste nodded soberly, "Much of the castle is, is it not, on one pretext or another? Let's look inside the door." It resisted and Andres applied another of his glittering instruments to it. The door swung open, revealing a large gray chamber with no windows and no other doors. The walls were perfectly smooth and the room was without any furniture. Around the walls stood a dozen or so women, some in the dress of court ladies, others garbed as upper servants. All the faces were familiar; women I was used to seeing about the castle. Droste stepped over to the nearest, sprayed at the hairline and lifted the hair to reveal a blue dome. A flap of skinlike stuff peeled away from the forehead, revealing the blue.

"These are what are called 'gynos,' " said Droste quietly. "They're replicas of real women, and a great deal more detailed physically than a GP andro like the servitors. Ordinarily they're only used for, well, rather discreditable purposes. Some of the male courtiers are probably from similar sources, but women generally have more sense than to . . . well it does happen though. But probably some of them are custom-made, both male and female. The resources of a good-sized planet were open to the people who constructed this place. If you'll come out onto the battlements with me I'll show you more." As I followed him out into the hallway he said, "There are no children here, are there?"

I shook my head. "We sent them away when the firedrake came. They don't seem to fly across the river. That's why the Castle is so empty, my father didn't want to separate families more than could be helped . . ." My voice died away.

Justinian Droste said dryly, "There's very little call for child-size andros, and no tapes for childlike behavior. Their resources weren't unlimited. Speaking of the, ah, firedrakes, how many have you seen close up at one time? More than one?" I shook my head and Droste nodded. "We only found one," he said. "*That* must have been custom-made. Someone had done it quite a bit of damage, though. Ah, here's the way out onto the battlements. Do you notice anything odd?"

I looked around me at the familiar scene. Around the horizon were the circling mountains; below us at the foot of the Castle Crag were the huts and cottages of Thorn village. Across the valley was what was now being called the Mount of Sacrifice, a name of ill-omen. But that was . . . Suddenly something about the clouds struck me. There was almost always a wind at Castle Thorn, especially at this time of year. I had hardly ever seen the clouds completely still at Thorn, even in midsummer. But now the clouds were utterly motionless, as if on a blazing day in midsummer.

"We're underground here, King Casmir," said Droste's voice in my ear. "The sky and clouds are holographic projections; so is most of the more distant scenery. Normally the cloud movement would be following a taped program but the little gadget that Andres is taking care of so assiduously stops all motion which depends on—well, certain electronic processes which are rather basic. I take it that you've been able to leave the castle very little and on those occasions you'll have gone north or roughly east."

At my stupefied look he shrugged lightly. "Those are side caverns," he said, "some of the scenery there is real. Any other direction you'd soon run into rock."

"But when I was a boy I ranged all over the countryside," I burst out. "It's only the last two years that we've been hemmed in like this."

Droste's tone was less somber as he said, "Two years, yes. That seems to be the time that this has been going on. Before that your memories are probably genuine, though they've been tampered with."

The state of shocked lethargy gave way to a surge of hope. "Then all this is just some sort of spell cast over me for the last two years?" I asked. "Of course, that's when Mortifer came with his warning of the firedrakes. When they came as he predicted my father would hear nothing against him. But I never trusted him . . . What did he do—kidnap me and imprison me here? The kingdom . . . my father . . . are they . . . ?" Hope died as I saw the look on Droste's face. I swallowed a lump in my throat and faltered. "In some of the old tales they say that men taken under the hills by the elvish folk have returned to find their friends grown old or dead; that a year with them under the hills is many years in the world of mortals. Is it . . . something like that?"

"Not quite, perhaps," said Droste gently. "But as nearly that as you're ready to hear now, I think."

"How long?" I asked, making my voice as strong as I could.

Droste's eyes met mine as he said quietly, "As nearly as we can tell from the time of your last genuine memory until now is about five hundred years."

11. A Double Tale

After that I was too dazed to put up much resistance to what they asked of me. I followed the man named Justinian Droste to a part of the battlements which, because it overlooked the Ladies Court, was normally forbidden to bachelor knights. A sort of bridge made of some grey metallic substance extended from the battlements to . . . I rubbed my eyes and looked again. A long arrow's flight away there was a jagged hole in the sky itself, and the metal bridge disappeared into it! Beyond the hole there was a gray-walled corridor which reminded me of the room in which the immobile "court ladies" had stood.

"Block out the bridge and the gap with your hand, then take it away," said Droste quietly. "Then you'll get some idea of the tricks of perspective which they used in building this place." I did as he said. When my hand covered the bridge and the hole I seemed to be looking out into a broad vista of mountains beyond the valley in which Castle Crag stood. But when I took my hand away I could see that the sky and mountains were some sort of picture, marvelously done, and that a strongly shot arrow could easily have struck that "sky."

The bridge was narrow but steady as a rock as I put my foot on it. "You wish me to go this way?" I asked Droste, and he nodded. Half expecting to fall through the bridge or find myself in some unimaginable heaven or hell when I had crossed it, I walked over the bridge, with only a glance at what seemed to be the abyss below me. I have always had a good head for heights, but the feeling that I was in a waking dream helped take away any apprehension I might have felt at the strange bridge and its impossible terminus.

The "sky" seemed to be made of some translucent stuff, some of which lay in shards on the floor of the gray corridor. I picked up a shard and looked at it, feeling as if I were a child in a nursery-story dream. The corridor itself was drably utilitarian, with smooth gray walls and a slightly resilient floor of somewhat darker gray. Droste came over the bridge behind me and walked along by my side. After a long stretch of corridor we came to a great circular space larger than the inside of the castle keep. Above us there was no roof; we stood as if at the bottom of a great well. The circle of blue high above was no larger than a shield. "That's the real sky," said Droste.

In the middle of the circular space were two great metal discs on which stood glittering machines and chairs which looked luxuriously soft. Seated in a chair near the center of the disc was a woman in close-fitting garments like Droste's; she faced a glittering array of lights and switches on a sort of table before her. As we walked toward the disc she turned toward us, and her whole chair swiveled to match her movement; a minor marvel, but one which startled me more than some of the greater marvels I had seen. "Citizen Droste?" she said sharply, seeing my sword; her hands moved sharply toward one part of the array of lights and switches before her.

"It's all right," said Droste reassuringly and I felt a small spurt of amusement as I realized that the woman must have thought that I had taken Droste captive. In fact, I was captive, not to his weapons, for he had shown none, but to my own ignorance. Until I knew more—much more—I did not dare to take action. But time and observation are great healers of ignorance; I could wait.

Droste waved me courteously to a seat on the platform and said to the woman, "Take us on in to the city; General Hospital. Andres will take the rest of the party back on the cargo disc." The woman looked a little dubiously at my sword, which I had laid across my knees for lack of a better place to put it, but gave a sort of salute and busied herself at her table. Suddenly I realized that the ground had dropped away and that we were rising in the shaft like a bucket in the well I had likened it to.

As we cleared the rim of the shaft I saw about me low arid hills and scrubby vegetation. We continued to rise until we were high above the hills, with the mouth of the shaft we had come out of only a small dark circle. Then the platform began to move smoothly and silently above the ground. We were moving away from the sun, which if this new world was anything like the one I was used to, meant that we were going east or west. But the dry desert landscape and clear sky gave me no hint whether it was morning or evening.

Presently I could see ahead of us what I thought at first was a curious group of mountain peaks. Then a certain regularity of shape and arrangement told me that these were monstrous buildings; each not only bigger than Castle Thorn but bigger than Castle Crag, Castle Thorn and all. There seemed to be parks and gardens at the foot of the towers, and one great stretch of what seemed to be greensward, looking oddly out of place in the desert setting. The woman spoke into the air as we approached the towers and was answered by a disembodied voice. Her hands played among the levers on her table and she said to Droste, "We'll have to loop around the starport; a starship is lifting and their GE fields can interfere even at this distance; it's a big cargo ship."

Droste nodded and leaned forward to look at the stretch of greensward, which we were now swerving to pass on our right. From the green area a gigantic black disc began to rise into the air. As it rose I thought that I could feel a faint tremor in our own flight, but that was soon gone as the black disc rose higher and higher until it dwindled into a dot in the sky. "Ever want to flit?" Droste asked the woman.

She shook her head with a smile. "Home is good enough for me," she said. "The operational height of this little buggy is as far as I want to get from Mother Earth."

Droste smiled back at her and turned to me. "You're

coming out into a wider world in more senses than one, King Casmir," he said. "Wider than you can know now."

I laughed shortly. "So it would seem, ser," I said. "No need to call me King, though; it is clear enough that my kingdom down under the hills was only a mummery, and my true throne gone to others these many years. The family name of the lords of Thorn is Jagellon; that, I suppose, is still mine."

"Indeed," said Droste with a curious note in his voice. Could it be pity? But he went on in a serious tone. "You know better than I what you have lost," he said. "But there is plenty for you to thank the Mercy for. I've seen other people from pre-tech societies meet our modern gadgetry for the first time and show everything from panic, fear to religious awe, to retreat into insanity. And it's worse for you because of the way you've been deceived for the past two years and the sudden way you learned of it. But you've hardly turned a hair."

It was an odd phrase but I could see that he meant that I had shown no sign of fear or amazement. What else, I wondered, did he expect from a knight of Thorn? But perhaps he knew as little of the knights of Thorn as I of what he termed "gadgetry."

I tried to keep that impassivity he had praised as our flying disc rushed toward one of the great towers, lifting at the last possible moment to come to rest on a broad flat roof at the top of the tower. As the woman dropped her hands from her table of lights she cast me a glance; I thought that in her own way she had been testing my courage. I grinned at her and she was startled into an answering smile. I heard and felt a brisk breeze blowing at the top of the tower and realized that a sort of barely perceivable thickening of the air which had surrounded our disc in flight had now vanished.

"This is a hospital, a place of healing," said Droste. "With your permission our Healers will give you a quick going over and see what sort of shape you're in. You show the signs of freshly healed hurts." I nodded without showing any emotion, but a sudden stab of hope shot through me. Whatever these people were, enchanters or something else, they seemed to have powers that would have been called magical in Carpathia. Their healing arts must be well advanced beyond anything known in my homeland. Perhaps, perhaps they could heal me of the Falling Sickness and make me a whole man again. I had often thought that I would trade my kingdom for freedom from the Falling Sickness; perhaps my wish had been strangely granted.

I followed Droste over to a part of the roof that seemed no different from the rest except that it had a large circle painted on it. We came to a halt and I looked at Droste in puzzlement, but suddenly the part of the roof within the circle flashed white and then began to sink slowly. I could not quite check an instinctive movement and Droste said quietly, "Just another means of transportation. It will take us down to the examining room." I nodded and rested my hands on the hilt of my sword, noting as I did so that the sword point went a little way into the material below my feet. Perhaps at need I could hack my way out of any place I wanted free of.

But when the sinking circle stopped in a room filled with more gleaming objects across which lights flashed I was faced with a small woman with an untidy mop of gray hair, clothed in a close-fitting white garment. "Please put the sword and your outer garments on the table there and come over to the examination area," she said crisply, and I obeyed meekly. She reminded me strongly of my old nurse and I could imagine her reaction if I demanded to keep my sword.

The "examining area" was another circle on the floor, but this one did not move. I stood within it and my skin tingled, then turned hot and cold as the gray-haired woman moved from one to another of the small tables and chests which ringed the circle on which I stood. Another woman dressed in white came from somewhere else in the room and looked at me in surprise. I concealed my own surprise, for her skin was darker than that of an old herdsman burned by the suns of many summers, and her hair was a mass of tightly coiled black ringlets. After the first surprise of her appearance I found her beautiful in her own way and I gave her a smile. She smiled back and said, "Hello, Casmir."

"Perhaps you'd better tell him how you happen to know his name," said Justinian Droste, who had been standing in the background.

The dark woman said, "We met about a month ago when I was on night duty at Central Receiving Hospital in Alba Cirque. He hadn't seen a dark-skinned person before and we talked a little about that. He was a bit worried about a history of what sounded like epileptic seizures, but from the nerve-path scarring it looked as if someone had used a neural interrupter on him repeatedly over a period of a couple of years. They were treating him with Lysergol and the scarring should be . . . Oh!"

She was looking at the surface of one of the tables and her face was troubled. "The scarring is back, as bad as ever!" she said. "I don't see how that's possible, in fact I'd say it was medically *im*possible. Unless . . ." She looked at me with a question in her eyes.

"No, my Lady," I said. "I have not seen you before—to my loss." I turned to Droste, "It seems that I have a double," I told him.

He nodded, his face grim. "Not only you but the whole setup in which we found you." Some things which he and the man called Andres had said flashed through my mind: "The same man," Andres had said, and Droste had spoken of a map of "the other place" as a guide to Castle Thorn.

There was an indrawn breath from the dark woman and she said softly, "The Mortifer case!"

I caught her eyes and spoke gently, but with authority. "You have guessed something, Lady. Can you riddle me this riddle?"

She looked gravely into my eyes and said, "You and the man I met must be clones, duplicates grown from the cells of a prototype. There are new techniques for retrieving memories from the cellular record of the prototype; that was what

Academician Mortifer was experimenting with, from the reports I've heard. Experiments have been done on animals but experimentation on humans is strictly forbidden by commonwealth law, and clones have the same rights as naturalborns." Her eyes went to Droste. "You're Justinian Droste, aren't you?" she asked, "of the Citizen's Liberties Union? Your group tracked down Mortifer's experiments and denounced him to the authorities."

Droste nodded and turned to me. "You had to know sooner or later," he said, "and perhaps this is as good a way as any. Our group, as Nurse Nerere says, is opposed to experimentation on human beings—or sapient beings of any species for that matter. Most attempts at such experimentation need rather elaborate technological support; we have ways of getting to know about such things. Not long ago we got on the track of Mortifer's experiments. First we found the first cavern, with your double and an identical setup to the one we took you from. We arrived at a rather dramatic moment, in fact."

He hesitated, then went on. "I'll tell you about that another time. Anyway, we investigated the setup and found some rather curious relay equipment. Eventually we traced the relays and found your cavern. There don't seem to be any more. So far as I can tell, Mortifer had set up two identical men in identical surroundings and was subjecting them to identical stimuli. What he hoped to prove I'm not sure."

I looked at my hands, at what I could see of my body. "Then I am . . . a . . . a homunculus?" I asked. "Made by Mortifer in the image of some real man?" My voice I think I kept steady, but only with a tremendous effort.

"No," said the dark woman fiercely, "you're as human as any of us; you've just been birthed by a more elaborate process. Ordinary conception uses cells from both parents; your cells are taken only from your prototype. But *his* cells contain genetic coding from two parents. Probably the most sensible way to look at it is that you, your double and your prototype are identical triplets, except that the prototype was born first and by more traditional means."

"Your humanity is recognized by the Commonwealth," said Droste, "and I'll soon give you evidence of that. For that matter it's recognized by the church your prototype belonged to, if that matters to you. It would have to him; he was a devout man by all accounts. But Mortifer might have interfered with those memories; it would fit what I know of the man."

I was calmer now, not only because of their words but because I was realizing that no matter what my birth I was alive and in possession of my powers. Then another dismaying thought struck me. "My . . . prototype . . . he must be . . ."

Droste nodded and said calmly, "Dead these five hundred years. But before he died he unified Carpathia; he's remembered as the greatest of their kings. And your double gave signs of some rather unusual talents before he disappeared."

I gazed at him in consternation, suddenly realizing how much I had been looking forward to seeing my other self. "Disappeared?" I said.

Droste nodded. "He left Central Receiving soon after Nurse Nerere talked to him. At first we thought he'd been kidnapped, but it seems he foiled a kidnap attempt on his own and went . . . exploring . . . We've traced him as far as Carpathia, the real Carpathia. But the trail ends there; he seems to have vanished completely after the destruction of Mortifer's laboratory."

12. The Jagellon Gift

I glanced sharply at Droste. "Mortifer is a man of these times then?" I asked.

Droste shrugged. "Perhaps of these times *and* the times of Casmir the Tenth," he said. "There's a Mortifer in many of the old tales and legends of Carpathia. It may just be a family name, but there seems to be no record of a young Mortifer or a father and son Mortifer alive at the same time. We have techniques for extending life; what's popularly called Life-stretch. The ordinary limit is about three hundred years, but Mortifer knows a lot about the life sciences. Perhaps he's found a way to extend his own life even longer; perhaps he's even cloned himself and transferred memories. We just don't know."

"So the Mortifer I remember . . ." I said slowly.

"May be a mixture of memories of the 'original' Mortifer and the one alive today, if they aren't the same man," said Droste. "But there's one further complication. As far as we can guess as to what he was up to Mortifer's plan must have involved giving you and your double the same experiences at the same times. When you and your double both saw Mortifer at least one of them must have been an android. There's something called a repeating android, which is a duplicate of a human keyed to exactly duplicate the actions taken by that human. A ruler who feared assassination might have a duplicate throne room built, hidden away somewhere. In the hidden room he might interact with holovision pictures of the people in the real room; they would see the android do just the actions the ruler was performing. But if an assassin torched the android the ruler would be unharmed."

"So Mortifer, too, has a double," I said slowly, as my mind raced over the possible complications of this.

"Perhaps not any longer," said Droste. "We found the remains of a repeating android in the ruins of Mortifer's laboratory. Perhaps he has another up his sleeve though; he certainly has enough accumulated wealth and expertise to build a dozen of them. His duplicates, however, can only do what the real Mortifer is doing. Your double is another human being, very much like you but free and independent. Even if it's true, as some claim, that clones given identical stimuli would act the same, he's had thirty days of experiences you haven't had. But I'm inclined myself to believe that clones are individual persons who could react differently even given the same history and environment."

"Be that as it may," I said. "I have a good idea of what my double is doing now. He pursued Mortifer to—what did you call it?—his laboratory. When he found only this duplicating thing you told me of I think that he must have continued to pursue the real Mortifer. Find Mortifer and you'll find the other Casmir not far behind him, I suspect."

Justinian Droste gave me a wry smile. "We've been hunting Mortifer ever since we first had evidence of his experiments," he said. "Your double had better luck than we did. My best plan now is to give you every assistance I can and let you see if you can duplicate the success of the other Casmir. And may the Mercy help Mortifer if either of you catch him! First things first though." He turned to the gray-haired woman. "Does he need any treatment?" he asked.

The woman surveyed me with a disgruntled air. "Oh, he's healthy enough," she said. "I've seldom seen a better physical specimen. I'd like to give him an injection of Lysergol for that nerve-path scarring. Normally it's not policy to let anyone with that in their blood out of custody since the Lysergol will inhibit the action of a neural interrupter. In this case I presume that's something of an advantage."

I looked to the dark woman for an explanation and she did not fail me. "A neural interrupter is a device which can render you unconscious; our peace officers use it for social control. Both you and your double have had one used on you repeatedly. I suspect that Mortifer simply rendered you unconscious when something started to go wrong in his experiments. That would account for the 'falling sickness' that the other Casmir described. As I told him, there's no organic reason for you to suffer fainting spells."

My heart leaped; this made up for much. "My thanks, Lady," I said. "When my quest is done I would like to thank you more adequately." I turned to Droste. "This land is strange to me," I told him. "I'll find Mortifer but it will be quicker if you help."

He nodded. "You'll have all the help that the Citizen's Liberty Union can give you," he said, "and to begin with, I'd like to register you as a citizen of the Commonwealth. It obliges you to keep our laws. But I think you'll find those simple and reasonable enough. In return you'll have the privileges of a citizen, which include a basic allowance of credit for food and other necessities. Anything beyond that you'll have to earn by your own efforts. But I have the authority to put you on staff as a temporary investigator for the C.L.U.; we can cover your expenses and even pay you a modest wage. By the time you find Mortifer I suspect you will have found a place in our society that you want to occupy."

I hesitated but then agreed. I knew nothing of the laws of this land and perhaps it was rash to agree to obey them, but from what I have seen of Droste and the others they seemed decent folk; I thought that I could live by the laws they lived by. I was asked to put my hand on a gray box and repeat my name. "Casmir the King . . ." I began, then stopped, remembering what my kingdom consisted of. "Casmir T. King," said a voice from the box. Then a light flashed and the voice said, "Duplicate file, Casmir F. Thorn."

"I could have told you that," said the gray-haired woman.

"The C and C chip keys on the genotype; when I worked in Maternity we always had trouble recording identical twins. The simplest thing to do immediately is to key it as a lost chip replacement until you can get it straightened out with Central." Droste nodded and she did something to the box that caused the light to go out. I felt a faint tingle on my wrist and when I raised my hand from the box I found a circular patch of blue on my wrist.

The dark woman came to my aid again. "It's just a patch of stuff that sticks to your skin," she said. "Move it around to avoid skin irritation. If you want to buy anything you'll put your patch in contact with a terminal and credit will be transferred from your personal account. Any credit you earn will probably be transferred directly to your account. The color of the patch indicates your credit balance. Green is normal; yellow and orange indicate increasing depletion of the account and red means that you're broke. Blue, indigo and violet indicate increasing credit surplus. Since yours is blue I presume that the C.L.U. has already credited you for the job they want you to do . . ."

"No," broke in Droste, "we haven't." He gave a short laugh. "Since this is a duplicate chip that must mean that the other Casmir has earned a credit surplus somehow. Furthermore that credit surplus was either originated here at Home or else a surcharge was paid to post it in Central Credit. I think we can stop worrying about your double, 'Casmir King'; he seems to be doing very well in our society."

Before they let me go free from the "hospital" they held a thing to my arm which they said would put a healing liquid in my blood and subjected me to a few more of their glittering boxes. I used the opportunity to find that the dark woman's name was Molly Nerere and that she could always be reached through Central Receiving Hospital in Alba Cirque. At last I was allowed to leave with Droste; we ascended again to the roof and took our flying disc again to another monstrous building. Another sinking disc took us to a corridor with several doors. At Droste's instruction I pressed my wrist with its colored patch on a shining metallic plaque near one door. The door flashed white and vanished and we walked into a room with a bed, table and chairs, decorated in muted colors.

"This is a fairly standard transient hostel room," said Droste. "You can pay more for something more luxurious if you like but that's on your personal credit; the C.L.U. will credit your account to cover this." He moved about the room, showing me how to get food from a niche in the wall and cleanse myself in what he called the "convenience." "If I were you I'd rest for a while," Droste told me. "The oval patch on the wall is called a View; if you press the contact on the bed frame there it will show you pictures that you may find interesting. It's for entertainment more than for education but you can learn quite a bit from watching it. I'll be back in the morning with what information I can get on Mortifer and on 'Casmir Thorn.' You're certainly free to leave the room and wander around the city but I think you may have had enough culture shock for one day."

I was suddenly conscious of a great weariness. As soon as Droste left me I flung myself on the bed and fell asleep almost immediately, though my dreams were troubled. When I awoke I broke my fast to the accompaniment of music and a picture of a rushing mountain stream; the result of my first experiment with the "View." It made me long for the woods of my boyhood, or rather, I realized, the boyhood of King Casmir the Tenth of Carpathia.

I thought of leaving the room then but the thought of the mistakes I might make in finding my way about discouraged me. Instead I began to see what I could learn from the "View." The solid-looking, marvelously realistic pictures it showed soon fascinated me and when Droste returned he found me propped up on the bed watching the pictures.

He laughed when he saw what I was watching. "They call those 'soaps' for some reason," he said. "They're dramas of domestic life; a very good choice for learning some everyday things about our society. I can't get over how quickly both you and the other Casmir have adapted yourself to our society. Ability to adapt is one component of intelligence of course, but it's more than that. Most people are strongly conditioned by their culture; they expect things to go a certain way and react with confusion or hostility if things aren't as they expect."

I shrugged. "The change from my old life was so drastic and so sudden that there was no choice except to learn quickly and to seize every opportunity," I said.

Droste laughed again. "Well, your double certainly seized every opportunity. So far as we can reconstruct his adventures this is what happened; an attempt was made to kidnap him from the hospital in Alba Cirque by a man disguised as an android by wearing a blue cap that simulated the blue dome of an android control unit. The other Casmir overpowered the kidnapper and left him in his own hospital bed, then made his way out of the hospital. Then somehow he hooked up with a rather criminal type named Joseph Pellow who was also disguised as an android. Apparently Pellow was attempting to spy on or steal from a rich merchant, Flavia Lorne, by using the android disguise. However, Lorne is none too honest herself; she involved your double in a scheme to impersonate her cousin. She was on the brink of financial ruin and the idea was to convince her creditors that her wealthy cousin was on good terms with her and would back her financially. The other Casmir used his impersonation to make friends with a wealthy trader named Benton who is an enthusiast for hunting wild animals. The other Casmir so impressed Benton and his sister Mirianne that they used their business connections to get him starpassage to Carpathia. Have you realized, Casmir, that the real Carpathia is a world circling another star?"

I nodded somberly. "Putting together some half-legendary lore preserved by the Knights of Thorn with what I've seen on the View, I've realized that this is not the world I remember. In fact, it can only be Earth, the place where the human race originated."

Justinian Droste looked at me in amazement. "No wonder

your prototype was able to unify a planet; your ability to make use of scraps of information is truly extraordinary. Most people call this planet simply 'Home' now; a fashion that started in the colonies but spread back to Earth. Carpathia is what we call a 'terranorm' planet, very much like Earth, which is why it was colonized.''

''What happened to the other Casmir on Carpathia?'' I asked.

Droste shook his head, his face somber. ''We know very little,'' he said. ''He appeared one day at Castle Thorn and created considerable furor by taking a sword out of a lock field on the tomb of Casmir the Tenth. The lock field was keyed to Casmir the Tenth, so of course either you or your double could retrieve objects from it. Apparently your double used the sword to fight off some sort of attack prompted by Mortifer. Then an agent of Mortifer's, pretending to be a monitor—a peace officer—got him to go to Mortifer's laboratory, probably by trickery. A young scholar your double had befriended used the incident with the sword to raise a mob to try to rescue him from Mortifer. But when they broke into the laboratory the place looked as if it had been destroyed by a series of explosions and there was no sign of any human being; only the destroyed repeater android.''

I looked at Droste. ''And that's the end of the story?'' I asked. The story had told me one thing that Justinian Droste seemed to have missed. The other Casmir evidently had, and was putting to good use, the Jagellon gift for inspiring personal loyalty in people after a very brief contact. Each of the people the other Casmir had come into contact with had done everything in their power to help him. Some of them, no doubt, had convinced themselves that they were using the other Casmir for their own purposes, but all of them had served his purpose. Droste himself, if he but knew it, was serving me as well as if he had been my sworn man. The responsibility that goes with the Jagellon gift is to see that no one suffers by serving us.

Droste was speaking in reply to my last question. ''The

only person we haven't managed to contact is the captain of *Argo,* the starship that took your double to Carpathia. She's taken her ship on a trading tour of the more primitive worlds and there's no way to contact her without a tremendous expenditure of credit. The trail of both Mortifer and the other Casmir seems to end on Carpathia."

"So be it," I said. "To Carpathia I will go."

"Well, I suppose we can arrange that," said Droste with a show of reluctance. "You seem to be our only hope of catching up with Mortifer."

"Oh, I'll catch up with him," I said absently, remembering that Mortifer was one of the few men I had met who was able to resist the Jagellon gift. "But what happens then is less certain. When the boar turns to bay then he is most dangerous."

13. The Bridge

Star traveling is no great matter if you travel, as I traveled to Carpathia, as a passenger on a gigantic passenger and cargo ship. The physical and emotional effects of "flitting" had been carefully explained to me by Justinian Droste and I exercised my body strenuously in the place provided on the starship. It was little used, and most of my fellow passengers seemed to spend their time inactive in their cabins. There was a View in my cabin with a variety of stories in pictures; by watching those intended for children I increased considerably my knowledge of the age I found myself in.

Droste had warned me what to expect, and when we were landing and the View showed me the sprawling city which surrounds Castle Crag and the unchanged Castle Thorn, I was in emotional freeze. I had been instructed by Droste that most "emotional therapists" who visited starships on landing were worse than useless, but if by any chance there was a Caphellan among them it could probably free me from the emotional freeze immediately, especially if I had been physically active on the voyage. It turned out that one did come aboard and I secured its services.

The very sight of the creature was almost enough to release my emotions though I had seen nonhuman sapients on the View. It was like a skeleton loosely draped in motheaten fur. From its round head three pale blue eyes looked at me with what seemed to me to be insolence and I growled at the creature, "Well, do what you're paid for—if you can!" Suddenly I realized that I was *feeling*. Boredom and impatience flooded through me; the first emotion I had felt since we had entered quasi-space.

The creature blinked. I felt surprised and then realized I was feeling *its* surprise. Then waves of tranquil happiness engulfed me. "I beg your pardon," said the Caphellan. "You are extremely sensitive to emotion, for a human. I did not realize that you would pick up my impatience with a task I perform only to earn credit to support my studies at the Academy of Life Sciences here. Are you by any chance a human from Chrysenomia?"

"No," I replied with a smile. "I am of Carpathian stock. Tell me a little about the Academy."

The creature blinked and was silent for a moment, then it began to scuttle backwards out of the cabin. "You are sending out a very strong emotional binding," it said. "I do not choose to be subjected to it. Seek your information elsewhere." It was gone before I could say a word, and it had not collected its very substantial fee. I would gladly have paid twice the fee for the very valuable information it had given me; the Jagellon Gift could affect nonhumans too. Justinian Droste had told me that the Caphellans were what he called "empaths": they could sense the emotions of others and make others share their own emotions. It was not surprising that such a creature sensed the operation of the Jagellon Gift but the most significant thing was that it seemed to have no defense against it but retreat. Mortifer, though, seemed immune to the Gift, so others might well be; I had better not be overconfident.

Helped considerably by having watched a View sequence for children on "Your First Starflit," I got my gear from the purser and carried it to the starport transient hostel where I secured a room. Here the procedure was somewhat different than when Droste had helped me secure a room at the transient hostel on the planet I was beginning to think of as Home. Comparatively few people were able to travel from star to star, and the colored patches worked only on the planet on which you were registered. For a stiff fee you could transfer registration but most starflitters carried small golden circlets called ecus which were an interstellar medium of exchange. When I pressed one of these ecus to the plate beside the door of the hostel room its gold color faded and it became worthless. For the three days I had paid for I was the master of the room; it would open only to the touch of my thumb on the plate. Food and drink came with the room at no extra fee, but if I did not choose to use them I would receive no credit. The View sequence for children had explained all this at somewhat tedious length, but in emotional freeze I had felt no boredom, and I was glad for the information now.

Mortifer's quarters and "laboratory" had been at the Academy of Life Sciences, not an easy place for a layman to enter, from what Droste had told me. For that reason I had jumped at the chance that the Caphellan seemed to offer for an entrée. But that scheme had failed. My only other point of reference was Castle Thorn itself; I might as well start there. It was easy enough to get there; free tours ran from the hostel to the castle, using discs which skimmed the ground rather than flying through the air. Whether they could fly at need was one of the many things I needed to know more of.

Hats were little worn in these days, for most garments had hoods which could be unfolded from their collars at need. But some men and women wore hats for show if not for necessity, and when Justinian Droste had helped me to buy clothing I had selected a wide-brimmed affair which shaded my face and hid my hair. Anyone who looked closely at my face would identify me with the other Casmir, but I was safe from a casual glance. I had a healthy respect for Mortifer; whether or not he was himself lurking somewhere on Carpathia he would have spies on the lookout for me, I was sure. If I had been in Mortifer's position I would have given serious thought to ordering my spies to kill on sight anyone who looked like Casmir the Tenth. The hat was some slender protection against being cut down from a distance before I could recognize the danger.

Nevertheless, my nerves were on the stretch as I stepped

off of the transport disc beneath the walls of Castle Thorn. Mortifer knew that I existed and must have guessed that his enemies would find me and that I would be on his trail. It would be natural for him to set traps wherever I was likely to appear, and this place was one of the likeliest. Personal weapons were banned by law in this society; that would not stop Mortifer or his minions but it made it hard for me to defend myself. Fortunately knives and clubs were too primitive to be thought of as weapons by these people; I had a hunter's knife at my belt and carried a stout walking stick.

I caught a motion out of the corner of my eye and whirled, shifting my grip on the stick as a man ran toward me. But the face above the shabby robe was beaming with friendship. I relaxed; this could only be the young scholar whom the other Casmir had bound to him with the Gift. "Good ser," he panted, trying to catch his breath. "I knew that you'd return! They made me put the sword back eventually, but all Carpathia knows that you drew it from the stone. Everyone is singing the old songs and the membership of the Old Carpathian Society has tripled!"

I grinned at his enthusiasm and gave his shoulder a friendly squeeze; it felt thin and bony under the worn robe. "I hear that you raised a hue and cry to rescue me from Mortifer, ser scholar," I said.

He smiled bashfully. "Perhaps there was no need, ser, but when I saw the monitor's platform fly you straight across the valley to Mortifer's quarters I was sure that he meant you some harm. When we broke down the doors and found the destruction I thought sure that you'd been killed, but the scanners found no organic material at all, so I dared to hope. How in the name of the Mercy did you escape, ser?"

"It's a long tale," I said, wishing that I knew it myself. "What would happen if I drew that sword out again?"

The young scholar's face was bright with eagerness. "If only you would, ser," he cried. "The Old Carpathians have been making plans; they have the petition all ready to call a special election for Tribune of the People. If you carried that sword around the Old Town news would spread like a mountain fire and you'd be elected Tribune by acclamation. As Tribune you could call for a vote of the people on any matter before the Council, and people would respond, not ignore the elections as they've been doing when Mortifer's gang was manipulating things."

It was a mad proposal; what had I to do with the affairs of this strange new Carpathia? Still the thought of spoiling some schemes of Mortifer's was tempting; that might bring the fox out of his lair. And a position of power might help me to deal with Mortifer when I found him. But what responsibilities would this office of Tribune involve? What would I do if I had to pursue Mortifer somewhere away from Carpathia? In the end, it was the unquestioning devotion in the young scholar's face which decided me. "You're a mad folk to choose a man for office because of an old face and an old sword," I said, "but it suits me well to spoil Mortifer's schemes. Mad as it is, I'll do it."

"Come then, before anyone can interfere," said the scholar. "My name, ser, which I never had a chance to tell you, is Paul Sobeski. The Castle guides are on our side and I'll get one to send word to Society headquarters as soon as we have the sword."

"If the Castle guides are on our side, who might interfere?" I asked him.

Paul Sobeski gave me a sidelong look. "Well, ser, we found some strange things in Mortifer's quarters but we didn't find his body. What we did find was a repeating android, or the remains of one and they can't be controlled from too far away. So Mortifer must have been on Carpathia and probably even in Thorn when you were taken to his quarters. He's lain low since, because the people were howling for his blood after that incident. But even if he's not in Thorn some of his agents are. Some of them are in official positions; the woman who took you to him was a real monitor. I don't know how far Mortifer's party will go but they'll certainly try to put legal difficulties in your way about the sword. In theory I suppose that it's government property and if the Castle guards weren't a law unto themselves the government people would have insisted on locking it away or putting a guard over it."

He was leading me past a statue by the main gate and as I glanced up at it I saw that it had a face that might have been my father's face as he was when I was a boy. A moment later I realized that it was also the face that I saw in the mirror, my own face.

"By the Mercy, it gave me a turn when I first saw you standing and looking at that statue," said Sobeski. "I thought then that you were a Jagellon descendant through some illegitimate line. But when you pulled the sword from the stone . . ."

"I am a clone, taken from the cells of Casmir the Tenth," I told him. "I have many of his memories and perhaps a few of his gifts."

"By the Mercy!" said Paul Sobeski eagerly. "Then Casmir really has come again! A few of the Old Carpathians are so traditional that they won't like the clone part, but for most of us it will make it even better. It's good to have a leader who's the descendant of a great king, but to have a man identical with that king is glorious!" I thought to myself that though young Paul thought of me as "leader" probably the other Old Carpathian leaders were thinking "figurehead"—let them think so until it suited me to change their minds; it is always easier to use folk when they think they are using you.

We entered a small gate, passed through a little shop that sold models of the Castle and figurines intended to be Knights of Thorn, and came out into a familiar courtyard. "We'd best go straight to the Hall of Kings, ser," said Sobeski, leading me up to the battlements and along them to where a graceful wooden bridge spanned a dizzying gap over to a rocky crag crowned with a little chapel. That crag had always worried me; too close to the castle walls and a determined enemy could climb it and shoot arrows over the battlements. The chapel they had built on it made it worse, if anything; it could be seized and used to shelter the enemy. Then I reminded myself that my prototype had united Carpathia; no need since then to worry about Carpathian enemies attacking Castle Thorn, and the flying platforms of these days made a joke of walls and battlements.

We crossed the bridge and entered the chapel they called the Hall of Kings. It was, I saw, a mausoleum, with tombs of many kings and memorials to those whose bodies could not be brought here for burial. From the quarterings on the shields we passed I saw that the descendants of Casmir the Tenth had cannily intermarried with all of the old royal families of the former independent kingdoms. It was wise policy, but I wondered if the later kings had been very pleased with those wives as wives. Perhaps there was some reason for Paul Sobeski thinking that the later kings might have left illegitimate descendants.

We came to the tomb of my prototype, Casmir the Tenth. The sword stuck in the stone on its surface was not the workaday sword whose duplicate was with my gear at the transient hostel, but a magnificent ceremonial thing, the Coronation Sword. I recognized too the slab in which it was set. When my father had shown me its trick I had thought it a piece of sorcery; now I knew it for a device familiar in these days, a lock field. It looked like a block of dark stone, but to the person "keyed" to it the stone became as permeable as water. Any non-living object could be placed in the field and seem to sink into the "stone" and be sealed there. I wondered what had made my prototype leave the Coronation Sword half in and half out of the field, and why it had not been re-keyed to his son and his son's sons.

I touched the "stone" with one hand, as the other Casmir must instinctively have done, and then pulled the sword out of it. A great bell tolled twice somewhere above us. Paul Sobeski's face was puzzled. "It tolled once when you pulled it out before," he said, "and no one could discover what bell had rung or how it was operated."

I shrugged; some device of my prototype perhaps. Looking around me I saw a little knot of spectators at the bridge, mainly dignified looking men in garments that looked like the ceremonial dress of the Knights of Thorn. Each wore a medallion round his neck. "The Castle Guides, ser," said Paul. "They keep the tradition of the Knights of Thorn and they'll follow you unquestioningly once they learn who you are." I gave them the Knight's Salute with the great sword and walked toward them. They respectfully stepped back, leaving the bridge clear for me. As well they did, for as I came to the center of the bridge a purple light flashed from the back of the crowd. Paul Sobeski crumpled unconscious at my side and would have gone over the edge if I had not caught him. Before I could do anything more there was an even brighter flash and the roar of flames. The wooden bridge was on fire beneath me and a wall of flames flared between me and the safety of the battlements!

14. The Balcony

I snatched young Paul up into my arms and whirled toward the Hall of Kings, but whatever had set the bridge on fire had struck behind me too; I was trapped between two walls of flame. The bridge gave an ominous crack and seemed to sink slightly beneath us. Throwing Paul over my shoulder, I crouched, trying to visualize exactly the distance between me and the battlements as I had seen it before the flames sprung up. I yanked at the scholar's robe which the young Sobeski wore, pulling it away from the front of his body, which was protected by being against my shoulder. Using the material as a sort of shield over my face I plunged into the flames with a bound which carried me almost to the battlements. My feet crunched on wood already half charred and the stench of the burning cloth was in my nostrils. But with another leap I got close enough to the battlements to sprawl across them. Strong hands grasped Paul and myself and drew us over the battlements to safety.

The Castle Guards were crouching behind the battlements; evidently some danger still hovered in the air between the Castle proper and the Hall of Kings. One gray-haired guide was crouched at the entrance of the stairway, fumbling with something which I recognized as a crossbow. As soon as I had made sure that the other guides had beaten out the flames on my hair and clothing and were tending Paul Sobeski, I got across the intervening space with a rush and a tumbling roll and took the crossbow from his hands. He had it almost cranked up; I gave a few more turns and slipped the crank off and thrust it into my belt. I tested the quarrell with my fingers; it was firmly seated. I brought the stock to my shoulder, made sure that I had a proper grip and stood up, my eyes searching the sky. On a small platform hovering in the air was a man with a long tube in his hands; there was a small flame at the tip of the tube that grew longer as he swivelled it toward me. With one practiced movement I aimed and pulled the trigger, then dropped down again. Flame seared over my head, but before I had dropped I had seen the crossbow quarrell blossoming from the throat of the man on the platform. I raised my head cautiously and saw that the man was huddled on the floor of his flying platform, his fire weapon spouting aimlessly into the air as the platform revolved slowly. As I watched, the flame died and the platform hung in the air, rocking slightly. There were no other enemies in sight, and I handed the crossbow back to the guide with a smile.

He gave me the hand salute of the Knights of Thorn and said hoarsely, "Thank the Mercy that I remembered that this thing hung on the wall in the room below. I ran for it as soon as I saw that bastard start torching the bridge; but I could never have shot it as you did, and there was only the one arrow in it."

"Thanks to you for your quick wits," I said. "Perhaps it is a good omen that a weapon from the old times has conquered those of these times."

That raised a ragged laugh among the guides. One of them called, "One for Old Carpathia," and another cried, "Casmir's come again," at which they all gave a cheer. I saluted them and went to see to Paul Sobeski, who was sitting up, dazed and groaning. His hair, like mine, was singed, but the only severe burns were on the back of his legs, where his gown had not protected his legs. I realized that the back of my left hand which had held him over my shoulder, was smarting. A guide bearing a white box with a red cross on it applied a soothing salve to our burns and we were both soon much more comfortable. A guide respectfully handed me the Coronation Sword which I had dropped when I handed Paul over to the guides.

One of the guides, a well-fleshed man of middle years, said respectfully, "My lord, the Old Carpathian Party headquarters have been notified, but by your leave it's not safe to parade through the Old Town as the scholar suggested. There's a balcony on the North Wall which some of the last kings used to address the people and it has some modern safeguards against attack. The fire will draw a crowd to the Castle anyhow; if we close the gates and hang a Jagellon banner from the balcony, there should be a good crowd assembled there in no time."

"Well thought of," I told him. "See it done." He saluted and left and I turned to the remaining guides. "Is there clothing here from the time of my ancestors that could be worn without disrespect to the dead?" I asked them. "No crowns or emblems of royalty, mark you, but the court dress of a Knight of Thorn, bearing the Jagellon arms." Two guides looked at each other and nodded, then saluted and trotted off.

A young man, not in guide's dress, pushed through to me, gave an awkward bow and said, "Ser, the Committee has filed the proper notice for the special election of a Tribune. There are 3V crews on their way to record your statement to the electors and the vote will be taken after the evening news. Probably your only competition will be some of the perennial candidates who always file for everything going, but you have to get sixty percent of those who voted on the last issue. Luckily that's not very many; citizen participation has been low lately. Now there's the problem of citizenship; I presume you're not registered on Carpathia and unless your current registration is at Home . . ."

"My citizenship was registered at Home and has not been changed," I said.

The young man looked relieved. "Oh, that's all right then; anyone who is registered at Home can acquire Carpathian citizenship by a simple declaration of intention to reside on

Carpathia and obey local laws. It's an old privilege from colonial days. Umm . . . there's a fax here, ser, with some suggested remarks . . . since you're, er, not familiar with local conditions . . ."

I looked at the sheet full of rhetorical phrases and references to names about which I knew nothing, smiled politely at the young man, folded the sheet and put it into my pouch. "I thank you," I said, "but I think that I will make my own speech. You may tell the men who wish to record my 'statement' that I will be speaking to the people from the balcony on the North Wall. If that will not serve their turn I will speak to them afterwards. All of you have my leave to withdraw except the scholar Paul Sobeski." The young man from the Old Carpathians was reluctant to go, but he was tactfully surrounded and led away by the guides. I smiled to myself; it was good to have trusty men about me again.

I turned to Sobeski; "Paul," I said, "you have until the crowd gathers to tell me all that I must know of the Tribune's duties and what will give the people reason to put me in that office. I find it hard to believe that many of them care that much for the Jagellon line in these days. What grievances have they that a Tribune can relieve; what hope can I give them that I can in conscience pledge my honor to?"

Paul grinned. "You underestimate the power of the Jagellon legend," he said, "but there is plenty that a Tribune can do and many wrongs that you can truthfully promise to right. In theory we have a Direct Democracy; the people vote by keying their Views with their C and C chips. Supposedly all matters at general policy go to the people and only technical matters are decided by the elected Council. But if there's no Tribune the Council decides what is a policy matter and what is merely administrative. The present Council has been using that power to keep the real decisions out of the hands of the people."

"What particular evils have they done?" I asked.

Paul Sobeski frowned thoughtfully. "We don't have time to go into specifics, but basically it's the same old story that you find throughout human history. Szilar history too, for that matter, or the history of any aggressive species, though empathic species like the Caphellans have other sorts of problems. Anyway those in power build up their own little empires, using the machinery of government to get wealth and power for themselves and their toadies, while the ordinary citizen can't get justice against them. Actually, those in government who only want the luxuries of life are relatively harmless; the ones who do real harm are those who enjoy bullying others for the sense of power it gives them or those who have big plans for interfering with other people's lives. One thing that's caused a lot of resentment is the new Eugenics Code, regulating marriage and childbearing. It's said that Mortifer is behind that and that what he's really trying to do is to use the entire planet as an experimental laboratory to test out some theories of his about selective breeding."

Two Castle guides approached us with garments across their arms and waited deferentially just out of earshot. "That must be enough for the moment," I told Paul, "but we must speak more of this; stay near me and we will use the first opportunity." I signed the two guides to approach and put on the garments which they had brought me; a surcoat with the Jagellon eagle embroidered on the breast, ornamental boots, a sword-belt and scabbard for the Coronation sword, and a great cloak of imperial red. One of them had had the presence of mind to find a basin of water and a towel, and I cleansed myself a little before I dressed. The same man offered to find scissors and trim my singed hair, but I shook my head. "For now, let us show our battle scars," I told him with a smile.

"There's already a large crowd assembled, my lord," said the other guide, "and the 3V men have set up to record your speech from the balcony. I'd say that the crowd was getting a little impatient."

"I come," I said, and let myself be led through familiar corridors to a room that had once been a solar for the court ladies. The windows had been enlarged and a large stone balcony built out, looking over a stretch of lawn below the castle. The grass was crowded with a great mass of people looking expectantly up at the balcony, over the edge of which a great banner with the Jagellon eagle was hanging.

"There are built-in pickups for the 3V and also a great many hidden deferences for this area," said one of the guides. "Some of the last Jagellons had a great many enemies to contend with."

I nodded, but as I walked out onto the balcony I felt very exposed. No arrow could reach me here from the crowd, and I was still immune to the flashing purple light that rendered a man unconscious, but no doubt there were many weapons I had not dreamed of in this time and place. Then I forgot fear as I heard a great shout go up from the crowd as I appeared on the balcony. I stood in silence for a moment, trying to reach out for contact with them. There were a great many people there, but in many ways a crowd is but one man, as any leader knows.

"People of Carpathia," I said, and some device magnified my voice so that it could be heard by all of those below. "Men and women of Thorn. We have a common heritage and a common enemy, Mortifer the Academician." At his name there was a sort of growl from the crowd that lifted my hopes. "This man, who is trying to meddle with your lives for his 'experiments' also meddled with mine. He took flesh from the dead king, Casmir the Tenth, and from it he grew another man, myself, with Casmir's form and Casmir's memories. I will not say that I am Casmir, the tenth king of Carpathia, that great man lies buried in the Hall of Kings. But some of his knowledge and some of his gifts I do have, and I have his heart too, full of love for Carpathia." There was a great cheer at that; I had them in my hands.

"Mortifer intended to use me, to play with me for his sport and his instruction," I told them, "just as he has tried to use this whole world of Carpathia. Good friends have helped me get free of Mortifer; I and my friends would like to make you free of him too. You have an ancient and honorable office, that of Tribune of the People. Some who love Carpathia and its history have proposed me for that office . . ." There were so many cheers at this that I had to wait to make myself heard.

"I am told by those I trust," I went on, "that although in form the people rule Carpathia in truth you are at the mercy of many petty tyrants. If you make me your choice for Tribune, I will free you from these 'tyrants' and put the rule truly back into your hands." There were more cheers at this, and I thought of ending my speech, but there were a few moves that Mortifer might make which it would be wise to guard against.

"There will be those who say that I am no true man, since I was not born as most men are," I said, "but I have just come from Home, the birthplace of the human race, and those in authority there have given me the mark of citizenship." I held up my wrist so that they could see the blue dot. "But Carpathia is my place; I will always return here and always make my home here, whether or not you trust me with this responsibility." Again I was stopped by cheers.

"Subtle men may suggest that I am only a tool of Mortifer, a new trick to deceive you," I said. "As if he had need of any such trick, so firmly does he have you in his hands. But I tell you, and trusty men well known to you will bear me out, that Mortifer has not ceased to try to kill me since I set foot on this world. The ashes of the bridge to the Hall of Kings are still smoking, where Mortifer's man tried to burn me down as I came from reclaiming the sword put in the stone by Casmir the Tenth!" I drew the sword and held it up and the cheer seemed to shake the Castle.

"This sword and the garments I now wear are treasures of Carpathia, legacies to you from an earlier and perhaps a braver time," I said. "Think of me too, as a legacy from that old Carpathia. Use me, as I would use this sword, to defend justice and freedom!" The cheers went on and on, and I decided to leave it at that, but I had to return to the balcony three times to respond to the cheers before I thought it wise to go.

The portly middle-aged guide who seemed to be their chief leader came to me then and saluted. "My lord," he said, "I've taken the responsibility of clearing the Castle of everyone except the Guides and a few people from the Old Carpathian Party who would like to consult with you. We are the remnants of the old Knights of Thorn, ser, and we have some ancient rights in this place which have been little used for centuries. The guides, ser, the Knights, would like to give you the old Oath as our Commander, and offer you the Commander's quarters in the Castle for as long as you wish to make use of them. Once you're elected Tribune you'll have plenty of safeguards, but it's my advice that you stay here at least until you're elected. Mortifer can't get at you here without destroying the Castle, and even he would have trouble doing that."

I gave my assent and in the chapel of the Castle took their oaths and renewed my own. Then over a scratch meal I consulted with the Old Carpathians about what wrongs should be righted and how it could be done. An elderly woman who was the titular head of the party because of her Jagellon blood was the most helpful to me; the others still hoped, I think, to use me to advance their own schemes. "In theory the Tribune can't advance any legislation on his own," the woman told me, "but myself and a few other Old Carpathians are still Council members; you've only to tell us what you want proposed and we'll do it, then you can use your powers to take it to the people."

"*If* he's elected . . ." said one of the others, but just then one of the guides appeared at the door. I nodded permission for him to speak and he said resonantly, "My Lord Tribune, you have been elected with the greatest number of votes ever cast in Carpathia!"

15. The Island

Good rulers are long remembered, but there are few songs and stories about them, for the business of bringing peace and justice to a land is mostly hard work, which makes a poor story. With the aid of Wanda Jagellon, the woman who was titular head of the Old Carpathian Society and Ladislas Mankowitz, the Chief Guide of Castle Thorn, I managed to use the power of the Tribune to root out the worst of the abuses which had grown up. Time after time Wanda or one of the other Old Carpathians would rise in the Council to propose some needed change, and time after time I would judge, "Let go to the People," before the Council could vote it down. The streets of Thorn and other cities were empty after the time of the evening meal as the citizens watched the debates on their Views and keyed their voting contacts. Then there came the time for Council elections; the Old Carpathians swept the elections and the fight became more subtle. I had to keep the Old Carpathian Party from re-establishing Mortifer's tyranny with their folk instead of his. But at last we won that fight too.

Everywhere we had encountered tentacles of Mortifer's power; in the Council, in the Civil Service, in the academies. Some of his followers I won over, some I had to cast out of office or destroy politically, financially or even physically. My own life was constantly under threat; the Castle Guides became again the Knights of Thorn and the Tribune's bodyguard, recruiting younger men to do part of the job. The Guild of Scholars took over guide's duties in those parts of the Castle that the Knights and I were not using. Time and again we encountered Mortifer's agents or followers, but of Mortifer himself there was no sign. I was beginning to wonder if I should pass on the Tribune's office to Wanda or Ladislas and seek Mortifer off-world.

Then late one night, as I worked alone in my quarters a personal call came in on my View. We had established a special code for those who wished to speak to me privately; much information had reached me in that way from those who feared reprisal if they approached the Tribune in any other way. Because of that, the code was such that there was no way of discovering from what place the call originated. I was not completely surprised, then, when on this night the View showed me the saturnine countenance of Mortifer himself. I ignored his face and searched the background of the picture for any clue to his location. He was too clever for that; it was a gray-walled room that could have been any general utility room in any modern structure on Carpathia. The one thing that the call did tell me was that Mortifer was probably still on Thorn; there was no sign of the subtle clues which technicians had told me would mark a feed-in from off-planet.

"You have already spoiled many lifetimes of work, 'Casmir King,' " said Mortifer in a sneering tone. "I see that it is time that I dealt with you myself."

I looked back at him with as little expression as I could manage; this man knew me even better than I knew him, having spied on me in moments which I had thought were private; I wanted to give him no clues to my thoughts. I lifted an eyebrow and said as casually as I could, "Your agents have had no great success in 'dealing with me,' Mortifer. What more do you think that you can do?"

Mortifer gave a sardonic smile. "I know how your mind works, 'Casmir King,' " he said. "You want to get your hands on me and you will take risks to do it. For my own purposes it suits me to meet you face to face. I think that your vanity will make it hard for you to refuse that offer. Name a time and place where you think that neither of us can betray the other. I will meet you there and show my superiority to you by outwitting your precautions. Then you will be in my hands again, though you may believe that I will be in yours."

My mind raced, rejecting possibility after possibility, then I said slowly, "In the river at the foot of this crag there is a little island which has been left wild because of a tragedy which happened there many years ago. I will set guards on the banks who will permit nothing to come to that island from this time until midnight tomorrow night. At that time I will swim over from the shore to the island and wait for you. The guards will let one man, either swimming or, in deference to your age, in a wooden boat, land on that island after me. Screens will be set to prevent either of us taking any metal or any energy device onto the island. We will be face to face with only our bodies and our wits. The first of us to leave the island may pass freely where he wills; you have my word on that. Thus, you may come and parley and leave freely. Or you may come and try to kill me and leave in safety after you have done it. But the screens will keep you from sending an android in your place, since there are both metal and energy devices in an android. Does it content you?"

Mortifer's face was impassive, but I could tell from the way his eyes slitted that he was thinking. Then a little quirk at the corner of his mouth betrayed the fact that he was pleased. "Agreed," he said. "After midnight tomorrow." Then the image was gone.

I gave orders to have the island searched by men and machines and to have guards and screens set up on the banks. "Don't neglect any possibility," I told my men. "Look out for any openings under water, such as old sewers. If anything comes up or down that river except one lone human in a wooden boat or swimming take whatever measures are necessary to destroy or capture it. Let anyone who can think of a way to outwit these precautions discuss it with my bodyguard. If a way can be thought of countering the danger, do it without consulting me; only if you see some peril which cannot be countered should you tell me of it."

Mortifer undoubtedly had at least one scheme which pleased him enough to make him agree to my terms; before the time of our meeting he would undoubtedly have others in reserve. I was wagering that my strength and wit would be equal to anything which Mortifer could do alone and without arms. Some form of poison would perhaps be his safest trick, and I took thought about how he might try to infect me with it and how I could counter him. I would not put it past him to give himself some disease to pass on to me but if he could cure himself of it, surely I could be cured myself. Would he send an agent, or a clone from his own flesh infected with something incurable? That had to be thought of; I consulted with physicians as to what poison or disease he might use. They pumped me full of their potions and assured me that for a day or two I was proof against any poison or disease which could be spread by simple contact. Something in the bloodstream was another matter; if it came to a fight I would have to beware scratches or bites.

For my part I put great hope in one simple and secret weapon; the Jagellon Gift. There was a good chance that I had never met the real Mortifer in the flesh; that he had used two repeating androids, one at each replica of Castle Thorn. For surely to meet either myself or the other Casmir in the flesh while sending an android to the other would have meant a difference in his treatment of us which would have threatened his scheme of "everything the same," for the two of us. If he had met me only through the medium of an android then perhaps he was not an exception to the success of the Jagellon Gift, and I might be able to confuse him if not actually bend him to my will. But even apart from the Jagellon gift I had ensured that the surroundings of our meeting were more in the world I remembered than in this world of machines and energy devices that I lived in now. A primitive island offered many possibilities.

I swam over a little before midnight, so as to reach the island exactly at the stroke of twelve as it sounded from one of the churches in the city. Then I set to work to use every second until Mortifer arrived. Mortifer might know this island, might have studied maps and pictures of it with care, but I had played on this island as a boy and he would never know it as I knew it.

I had swum over in shirt and breeches with supple leather shoes tied round my neck with their own laces. I soon found the rocks that broke into sharp shards when properly tapped. On the third try I had a workable knife with which I cut myself a staff and a bow, stringing it with a bootlace. The other lace I used to tie sharp stone points onto the sturdy reeds I made into arrows. It was a stroke of luck that I found a shore bird's nest with some feathers in it and three eggs. With a grin I took the eggs and put them in a sack I improvised from my shirt-tail; they might make distracting missiles. I withdrew to a hollow in the rocky hill at the center of the island and watched the shore while I split the feathers and stuck them to my crude arrows with a glue improvised from birdlime and the white of an egg. The island was too high to climb on three sides; a swimmer or a man in a boat could only land on the shore within my field of view. So long as the sliver of moon was not obscured by clouds I had perfect observation of anything approaching that shore. When I had fletched the arrows I made a sling from my other shirt-tail and a few remaining bits of shoelace, then folded the tops of my boots down to hold them on comfortably without their laces.

I was now armed as well as I could arm myself quickly to keep Mortifer at a distance if it came to a combat. He would only fight me, I reckoned, if he had poison or some other device up his sleeve; even if he had been my equal at combat he would chance nothing on a fair fight. I had reckoned correctly that he would not come immediately, hoping to play on my nerves by the delay. When I had been younger and more impatient he had sometimes got under my guard by playing a waiting game and I had thought that he would try that trick again. I let myself relax, keeping only my senses on the stretch. I was aware of the smells of the island and the small, normal sounds of birds and little animals going about their nocturnal affairs. Suddenly there was the squawk of a sea bird and a splash. I grinned; there was one point on the cliffs where it looked as if they could be climbed, but many a skinned knee and knuckle had taught me that the appearance was illusionary. Still, five hundred years might have worn down even that hard rock; I did not relax again until the grumpy muttering of the sea bird assured me that the climber had given up that route. Without ignoring other possibilities I looked most often to the end of the beach nearest the cliff that my opponent had tried to climb. There were broken rocks there and a man swimming along the cliffs might use them as shelter to make a stealthy approach to the beach.

At last I caught a glimpse of a shadowy form among the rocks. As long as it stayed there I could see little of it, but eventually my opponent would have to land. After a long pause, during which he must have been surveying the island as best he could, I saw an oblong shadow drift into shore and heard the scrunch of gravel. Against the paler color of the beach I could see that it was an inflatable boat. By great good fortune one of my men had suggested that I use such a craft to save myself a swim and I had been curious enough to examine one. A thought struck me and I picked up an arrow and fitted it on the bow I had made. Such boats were normally inflated with air, but what was to prevent Mortifer from filling it with a noxious gas and releasing it against me unexpectedly? As soon as I saw the figure of a man slip away from the boat for the shelter of a rock I drew back the arrow and fired it at the inflatable boat.

At that distance with so large a target even my crude weapon could hardly miss. There was a loud hiss and the boat shriveled and dwindled. The dark figure on the beach ran frantically away from it and I thought that my guess had been a good one; if he merely feared another arrow he would have done better to stay behind his rock. "I said a wooden boat," I called softly and then quietly slid over the edge of my hollow into a little ravine beside it.

As well I did, for the figure on the beach raised his hand and there was a snapping sound and a missile of some sort hummed over my head into the hollow. A good try for a snap shot at a voice from the dark. I thought that what he had must be something like a small crossbow; the missile had buzzed like a crossbow quarrell. If that was so, he would need to reset it before he could fire again. I rose to my feet, swung my sling around my head once and let fly an egg at his position. There was a squelching sound as it hit and the dark figure plunged back into the sea. I grinned as I slid into another prepared position, a little closer to the beach. I had reckoned that my opponent's imagination would magnify a simple bird's egg into some noxious substance which he would try to wash off as quickly as possible.

He was indeed scrubbing at his skin where the egg had hit, then he plunged into the water again and swam a few strokes. But in a moment he rose to his feet, tossed something away from him and waded back into shore. A voice which could have been Mortifer's but which sounded different enough to put me on guard called out. "All right! First round to you, Casmir King! I am counting on the fact that you want to question me, not just kill me. I have no other weapons; come down to the beach and talk. If you do, I may answer some of your questions."

I trusted him not at all, but that was a powerful bait, as he knew it would be. "Walk over to the large rock to your right," I called, "and sit on it with your hands at your sides. I'll come down to you."

As I remembered, the rock was just a bit too high for even a tall man to sit on with his feet on the ground; my opponent had to perch on it with his feet dangling. From that position he could not come at me without a betraying movement to warn me. When he was sitting down I came softly down the hill and stepped out on the beach a short spearcast away from him. My bow and arrows I had dropped just short of the beach, my staff I held in my hand and my sling with a stone in it was tucked into my breeches in the back. "This will do for now," I said. "Now tell me, Mortifer, if Mortifer you be, what was the reason for your treatment of me; why the false Carpathia in the cavern, why the androids that looked like the folk of old?"

The figure on the beach shrugged. His face looked like Mortifer's from this distance but something about the body didn't fit. The voice, though, sounded more like Mortifer's when he spoke: "It was a controlled environment; I hoped to learn a good deal about the behavior of a born leader like yourself; perhaps things I could apply to my own purposes. But there was another reason too. Casmir the Tenth defeated my plans for him and then escaped me by dying. It amused me to make a reborn Casmir my experimental subject and eventually my tool."

"Your tool for what?" I asked as calmly as I could.

"Why, to rule Carpathia first and after that a wider realm," said the other man mockingly. "With the proper opportunities Casmir could have built an interstellar kingdom, not just united a planet. You've made a good start here 'Casmir King'; any day your puppets in the Council could propose a restoration of the monarchy with you as king and the people would pass the measure. Perhaps that's what I'll have 'Casmir King' do when he leaves this island."

"And how do you propose to make me do that?" I asked as mockingly as I could.

"Oh, not you," said the man on the rock, and put his hands to his head. He pulled something from his head and face and looked up at me with a smile. The smile was the crooked smile of Mortifer, but the face revealed in the moonlight was my own face!

16. The Ghost Hound

"Another clone, of course," said the man on the rock, "but with my memories instead of those of Casmir the Tenth. That proved—unfortunate—in your case. Besides that I've come to the conclusion that the factor I'm looking for is genetic; I can ignore Casmir's background and training."

"And the original Mortifer?" I asked softly.

The other man shrugged. "He still exists, so even if you killed this body, 'Casmir King,' you wouldn't have defeated me. But I'll kill you, of course, and then go back to your followers and take over what you've built up. I suppose that I'd better smash your face in or else someone might raise uncomfortable questions. A pity; I'd like to get you in the laboratory and take you apart carefully."

"You haven't got me yet, either to smash or to take apart," I said mockingly.

The other man gave a nasty laugh, all the more disconcerting because it was in my own voice. I realized that when he spoke it was the speech patterns and intonations that made him sound like Mortifer; the voice had always been mine.

"I can take you when I wish," he said. "Do you think that I'd set up an experiment without an emergency cutoff in case things went wrong? All I have to do is speak one word that will key a reflex I put into you in the tanks. Your breath, your heart, your whole involuntary nervous system will stop. Brain damage in a few moments, death in a few more; I won't even have to touch you. You can't possibly reach me in time to keep me from saying that one fatal word. So keep your distance my barbarian warrior; you don't have long to live in any case and I'd like to know a little more before I finish you."

I felt as if an icy hand were squeezing my guts, but I forced my wits to work. "And what happens to your body when that word is spoken?" I said softly. "Or even if that word won't kill you, isn't there another which will? Do you think that the original Mortifer will leave you alive after you've served his purposes? Let me help you get rid of *him* and let me live to help you. I'm in your hands if what you say is true; I could never be a threat to you. I'll do whatever you want, put on the mask of Mortifer you wore here and pretend to be your prisoner . . ." My hand groped frantically in the pouch behind me; if that nest was old enough the yolk of the eggs should be thick and glutinous. Would they do? They had to, there was nothing else I could get in time.

"No," said the other man, "I don't dare trust you . . ." I crunched the eggs in my hand and clapped my hands to my ears, filling my ear holes with a mess of yolk, white and shell. Yelling like a maniac I ran at the other man with my stick. His mouth was working but I could hear nothing, but an undifferentiated sound. I thrust at his throat with the sharpened end of my stick but he was as quick as I; he struck the stick aside and grabbed for me.

We grappled and rolled on the beach, bodies equally matched and skills of combat seemingly equal too. Several times he almost held me down, while he tried to shout in my ear. Every blow I could land went to his mouth, his throat, his diaphragm. He kneed me and I doubled over in pain, the flaked stone knife digging into my gut as I bent. We were too equally matched; I had to use that knife. I plucked it from my waistband and aimed up for his stomach, but a sudden wriggle of his body deflected my aim and I felt it slip between his ribs. Blood gushed and an expression of astonishment came over the face so like my face; the limbs relaxed. I thought it was a mortal blow, but I dared not trust him; my hand groped for a rock on the beach and I smashed his skull with it.

Before my blood could cool I hit again and again, obliterating his face as he had planned to obliterate mine.

I stumbled to the edge of the water and washed myself compulsively retching but unable to bring up anything. A fragment of an old verse ran through my mind:

> I fought a dead man on the shore
> And I think the man was me . . .

Presently my shuddering ceased and I walked back to look at the body, its head now a bloody mess. "Forgive me, brother," I said uselessly. From the moment I had known what he was I had known he had to die. He might have had the Jagellon gift, and the combination of that gift and Mortifer's mind was too dangerous to let loose in the world. But the necessity was bitter; another score against Mortifer. Had I committed suicide, fratricide or simple murder? I wondered. At any rate there was another death I must accomplish; it was too dangerous to parley with Mortifer any longer, or try to question him; I must kill him on sight.

I examined the body minutely, but it told me nothing. Was this yet a third clone or had Mortifer captured "Casmir Thorn," stolen his memories and replaced his mind with Mortifer's? There was no way that I could see of telling. What would have happened to this man eventually; would the Jagellon heritage have overcome the Mortifer memories given time enough? I wanted to think so, and that made this death yet more bitter. Wearily I made a rough cairn of beach rocks over the body, entered the water again and swam with slow strokes back to the place where I had gone into the river to swim to the island. Once ashore, I dispatched technical crews to the island, took a transport disc to the Castle and summoned my closest advisors.

"I met a duplicate of myself on the island," I told them bluntly. "Mortifer's plan was that the duplicate come back and take my place. Before we go any farther I want you each to question me about things that have happened since we met until you are absolutely sure that I am the man you elected Tribune."

Once the inquisition was over I told them the whole story of my encounter on the island and told them for the first time about "Casmir Thorn." Then I drew some morals. "I am vulnerable," I told them. "If the man on the island told the truth—and his behavior tells me he did—Mortifer can kill me any time that he can have one word spoken in my ear. I see no way of guarding against that; one of you might tell me tomorrow that a man named Rumplestiltskin had been trying to reach me and I might fall over dead before your eyes."

"Not necessarily," said Wanda Jagellon. "I was a nurse for a while before I got involved in politics and I'll wager that once the reflex is triggered you can be kept alive in a heart-lung field until a psychoneurologist can find the reflex and override it. I'll give orders to have a medical team with the right equipment standing by in the Castle."

"My thanks to you, Lady Wanda," I said with a lighter heart. "That makes the case less desperate, but still it restricts me to places where I can get such medical help quickly. Furthermore, Mortifer could strike me down at a moment of crisis and leave all in confusion. It is past time that we had another Tribune; will you take on the task, my lady?"

She nodded with a little smile. "The people will accept a Jagellon woman I think, but only as your deputy. I'll be the junior Tribune and take over if you are incapacitated."

"My thanks," I said. "It is no light burden that you take on, as well you know. The other problem, though, is what to do if Mortifer introduces another duplicate at some crucial moment. Mortifer has secret supporters still, and many resources. What if a duplicate appeared on the View with some lying tale? At best it would confuse the people and destroy confidence in us; at worst it might enable Mortifer to take over somehow."

Wanda frowned. "Your strictly legal powers depend on the Council being in session. Things are slow; we can keep the Council in recess for a while."

Paul Sobeski tapped his fingers on the table around which we sat. "What we need is some means of identifying you as yourself which a duplicate can't easily reproduce—or steal. The trouble is that all the means of identification in our society depend on genotypes and a clone would have the same genotype and key the same identity tests. And it has to be a publicly visible sign of identity. You could have a fire-drake tattooed on your chest and *we* would know that a duplicate without the tattoo wasn't you, but as soon as you publicize anything of that kind Mortifer could reproduce it on his clone."

"There are unique gems in the Treasury here at the Castle . . ." began Ladislas Mankowitz.

I shook my head. "I wouldn't put it past Mortifer to duplicate any material object. He duplicated Castle Thorn itself—twice! Anyway if we put our trust in something like that Mortifer has only to steal it somehow and it becomes a weapon against us."

Ladislas knit his brows. "Something alive?" he suggested tentatively. "A dog perhaps."

"Not a dog," I said. "Any duplicate would smell just as I do and I don't think a dog could tell us apart. The difference between me and a duplicate made by Mortifer would be in the mind and a dog can't smell your mind . . ."

"No," said Wanda softly, but with excitement, "not an ordinary dog. But a Caphellan ghost-hound can!" She turned to Ladislas. "Get on to the exotic importers, Ladislas. I doubt if there's a ghost-hound on Carpathia, so put in a special order. I'll use my personal credit to give Mortifer a little less chance of getting to us." She turned to me. "The Caphellans are extreme empaths . . ."

"Yes," I said. "I've met one."

"Good, then I don't need to explain the Caphellans," she said. "As you might guess they find it extremely painful to go among other species who have uncontrolled emotions by Caphellan standards. To a Caphellan you or I are constantly 'shouting' our emotions and are completely 'deaf' to the emotions of others. Imagine living among deaf people who constantly bawled at the top of their voices. So Caphellans living in other societies are extremely reclusive. At home Caphellans have little use for pets; they get constant emotional support from other Caphellans. An isolated Caphellan feels the lack of that support so they're bred a sub-sapient Caphellan life-form into a sort of a super-pet for Caphellans who have to live away from other Caphellans. They form a unique emotional bond with their master or mistress . . ."

I frowned. "I don't see why if I got such a creature Mortifer couldn't acquire one too and bond it to his duplicate."

Wanda smiled, "Ah, but you don't know the unique characteristics of a ghost hound. They sniff out hatred and fear; that should make it harder for a traitor to get near you. But most important they can detect when a person is lying. In particular, if its master lies a ghost-hound 'blushes'; turns a deep rich red all over." She added dryly, "They aren't popular pets among non-empaths."

"It may just work," I said slowly. "There's a Caphellan at the Academy, or was when I landed here on Carpathia. See if it has a ghost-hound and will cooperate in making some sort of presentation of it to me on the View. Don't cancel the order to the importers, Ladislas; even if the Caphellan parts with his beast I presume that it will want a replacement."

The Caphellan was located and agreed to trade us the ghost-hound for a round trip starpassage to Caphella. "In the emotional freeze of a starflit I won't miss my pet," the creature said, "and after restoring my soul by communion with my people I can bring back a young Lar, a "ghost-hound" as you call them. My own beast is getting rather old. Ordinarily it would not transfer its loyalties to a new owner, but in your case I think there will be no trouble." The Caphellan gave me an enigmatic glance from its three eyes and I remembered that it had been able to detect operation of the Jagellon Gift.

We had a rather impressive little ceremony broadcast on the View. The Caphellan presented me with his ghost-hound.

"I am returning to Caphella for a while and can find another," it said. "Your planet has been kind to me; I think that this will be for the good of your planet and your Tribune."

I thanked him and turned to face the receptors which sent out my image to the Views in homes and public buildings all over Carpathia. "I have never lied to you, so far as I remember," I said. "If I try to do so from now on, you will easily catch me out, for Trinka, my ghost-hound, will always be with me. If I do tell you a lie, see what happens." I thought for a moment and then said earnestly. "I am completely happy about never being able to tell a lie without Trinka giving me away." I grinned as a flood of red color flowed over Trinka's body from the tip of her nose to her feathery tail. It was a remarkable sight, for Trinka looked not unlike a white Afghan hound, but her fur was not hair but a sort of soft quills filled with liquid, which is what in fact changed color.

I looked into the receptors again. "Even an honest man does not like to *have* to tell the truth," I said. "The reason that I have accepted Trinka, and will keep her with me constantly, is that Mortifer, my enemy and yours, is still plotting against us. He has tried to kill me and will try again, and for that reason I am going to have to restrict my activities for a while. I ask you to give your votes to Wanda Jagellon as Second Tribune, so that she can help me with my duties and take over if Mortifer succeeds in putting me out of action. Mortifer may also try to substitute someone for me; someone who looks like me in every way, but is a creature of his own. So long as you see Trinka with me you will know that you can trust what I say if I warn you of a danger or ask you to take action. If you see me without my ghost-hound, beware! Even if it looks like me it may not be me." That should take care of the most obvious moves that Mortifer could make, having a duplicate commit some atrocity for instance to destroy my popularity. Better tell Ladislas not to cancel the order for another ghost-hound though; poor Trinka was probably a prime target for assassination now.

"I tell you most sincerely that Mortifer is a danger to Carpathia and even to the Commonwealth as well as to me. Any citizen who has information that might help us find him is urged to contact us at the Tribune's special code; for the time being that View will be manned by a team of operators who will record your information."

I looked into the receptors then and said softly, "Mortifer, kill me if you can, for if you do not I will put an end to you and your plans."

17. The Lake of the Crater

In the end it was a child and a clerk who led us to Mortifer. Paul Sobeski, who was acting as my secretary, had supervised the first sorting out of the flood of messages which followed my appeal for information about Mortifer. After over a week of work he came to me one day and said, "I'd like you to hear two record chips taken from the calls we got about Mortifer. Put together, I think that they might give us a valuable clue."

When the first chip was inserted in the playback it showed on the View an elderly woman with a precise, fussy air. "I am the chief dispatcher for the Central Chemical Concern," she said. "We used to supply the laboratory of Academician Mortifer at the Academy in Thorn. In dispatching one gets used to a certain pattern of supplies for a given customer; in many cases one could fill the order almost automatically. But there is enough judgment involved that the job can't be computerized. After the election of Our Tribune orders from the Mortifer laboratory ceased and I rather expected to have an overstock on some rare items. However, I've noticed that all of these items continue to be ordered. The orders are spread out between a dozen different customers, many of them new customers. Those who aren't new haven't ordered these particular items in the past. Put together the orders from those dozen firms almost exactly duplicate the typical order from the Mortifer laboratory. Most of the firms are east of the mountains, but when occasionally I get a rush order for an item it almost always goes west. Two special rush orders have gone to a rather odd location; a little town on the edge of Lake of the Crater Crown Preserve. My husband and I have vacationed in that Preserve; I can't think of any enterprise in that little town which could possibly use such chemicals."

She paused and blushed very slightly. "When I was a girl I used to be very fond of stories about King Casmir the Protector. When Our Tribune came to us . . . Well, I just wouldn't want anything to happen to Our Tribune. I used to respect Academician Mortifer, but if he is trying to kill Our Tribune he must be a very wicked man and he should be caught as soon as possible."

The playback ceased and I turned to Paul. "As soon as we have time I'd like to thank that woman in person, Paul," I said. "Wanda has offered me various family heirlooms from the time of Casmir the Tenth; see if you can find something among them that this woman might like and ask Wanda if she will give it to me to pass on to our informant as a token of appreciation."

Paul made a note with his pen on a pad of paper—a scholar's affectation in this day of recording chips—and said, "I'm sure she will. The next message is from a child; a boy who lives on a farm near that Crown Preserve."

The boy might have been a farm lad of my old times; sturdy, freckled, clad in a faded shirt. "Well, I don't know if this will be any help," his recorded image said, "but it's sure funny. We live just on the edge of Lake of the Crater Preserve. Us kids around here always used to swim in the Lake, and the rangers never said anything. But a couple of years ago the Preserve was pretty well closed down; they said the scientists from the Academy in Thorn were using the lake for experiments. When Dad tried to protest he didn't get anywhere; eventually he found out that Councillor Mortifer was behind these experiments and in those days, before Tribune Casmir came, you just couldn't buck old Mortifer."

He paused and spoke a little more awkwardly. "Well, us kids were mad, and we've been sneaking over at night and in the early mornings to swim. I'm sorry if we've been breaking the law but we didn't think it was fair. So anyway my friend Jimmy and I have seen some awfully funny stuff going on in that lake. They take boats out at night and drop big cases of stuff right into the water in the middle of the Lake. And we've seen transport discs going down into the water too, and one time we almost got caught when we were swimming and a transport disc came right out of the water. So since old Mortifer was behind getting the Lake closed I figure that maybe it was something Tribune Casmir oughta know. And . . . if this is some help to you, could you maybe see . . . about getting the Lake open again for swimming, Tribune?"

Paul and I both chuckled as the playback finished. "Once we had those two leads we did some further checking and found some other leads pointing to that location," said Paul. "We're pretty sure that it's a secret stronghold of Mortifer's; perhaps his main base now you've driven him underground. There's a good chance that he himself might be there. I'd like your permission to send in an assault team of monitors; the charges pending against Mortifer are serious enough to get us a search and seize warrant from the High Court of Justice."

I frowned. "If I know Mortifer he won't be taken easily; he probably has half a dozen escape routes. I think that our best chance is to intercept the next big shipment and get ourselves dropped into Mortifer's stronghold in some of these big crates the boy spoke of."

Paul sighed. "You say 'ourselves.' You *are* going to insist on going then?"

I grinned at him. "Did you doubt it?"

He smiled wryly back. "Not really. All right; the Tribune has certain powers of investigation which we can probably stretch to cover this. You're certainly as much an expert at hand-to-hand combat as most monitors, and they'll certainly follow you with enthusiasm. But take every precaution, Casmir. Carpathia is recovering nicely from Mortifer, but we'll need you around, at least as a symbol, for some time yet. Besides that, your friends would miss you."

"And I you," I said. "Don't worry, Paul. This new life is much too interesting to throw away recklessly. I'll wear earplugs against that 'magic word' of Mortifer's and take some other precautions, too. Ask the Healers if it's safe for the whole assault group to have Lysergol injections so we can't be knocked out by neural interruption. We'll carry those Fire Service shields against torching and wear regular monitor's body shields against projectiles. If we can get inside the defenses by being delivered like packages, I have hopes that those things will be enough."

Paul nodded. "Yes and you'd better wear Support Suits and carry a reasonable air supply too. That way if Mortifer floods the place or tries some sort of gas attack you'll be all right. In fact, with Support Suits you can be neatly sealed inside those cases and not have to be worried about air holes or what happens when they drop you in the Lake."

For all that, we were uncomfortable enough in our packing cases as the boat carried us over the surface of the Lake of the Crater. Some of us had been in those cases longer than others; we had tried to insert ourselves into Mortifer's supply chain as unobtrusively as possible, burglaring warehouses in the dead of night to substitute monitors for supplies. An "accident" involving a cargo disc had enabled us to substitute the last few cases in the confusion. Luckily Mortifer tended to use standard sized chests large enough, though barely, to hold a man. A few boxes too small to hold a monitor were packed with equipment we hoped would prove useful.

The sound of the engine that drove the boat ceased, and I heard clanking sounds through my packing case. Very careful observation from the shore by our agents had told us the routine that was followed; the boat was moored to a buoy tethered just below the surface and the cases were tipped overboard from the side of the boat, which then returned to a boathouse on the shore of the lake.

Presently, the case I was in was lifted and dropped into the water. I was head-down for a moment, then the case was righted by the weights which had been placed at my feet to make the case weigh the same amount as the one we had substituted it for. Presently, there was a bump and silence for a while. Then the case was pushed sideways for a way and there was another pause. A loud humming began and I felt myself descending again. Then there was a gurgle of water running away.

I moved aside a little hatch which had been built into my case and peered out through the piece of dark translucent material which, I hoped, concealed my spyhole. The cases were standing in a large circular chamber from which water was gradually draining; harsh white lights behind protective transparent panels lit the scene. When the water was gone a heavy round door opened in one wall and blue-domed androids with cargo handling equipment came into the room. I let them take a case or two to the door so that there was one case inside the door and another blocking it. Then I simultaneously keyed a machine I held and kicked the release that made my case fall away in two halves.

The androids froze, as they had at the false Castle Thorn when Droste and his men invaded it. I blew a blast on a whistle which I had carried on a chain round my neck and all of the cases carrying monitors split and spilled out their contents. Each man or woman ran to perform assigned tasks; making sure the door was well blocked so that it could not be closed on us, retrieving pieces of equipment from the smaller cases.

We formed up in skirmishing order and went down the corridor upon which the door opened. No effort had been made to close the door, though it was remotely, not manually, operated. Either our invasion had been unobserved or else the enemy was playing a waiting game. Reluctantly I keyed the contact that would turn off my sound receptors; from now on I must travel deaf and let others be my ears. We were all anonymous in dark-colored Support Suits, but Mortifer knew me well enough to realize that I would want to be in the assault group myself. If he spoke the word that would stop my heart and breath there might be no time for my companions to aid me, even though one of them was a Healer and carried emergency medical equipment.

The monitors carried equipment to override any ordinary door lock and we left no room unexplored as we passed along the corridor. This was a storage and service area; one room held neat stacks of supplies, another a transport disc in the process of repair. There were stored foods in some rooms and one was a wine cellar. Mortifer, I remembered, prided himself on his discriminating palate for wine, and since he was not a man to indulge his servants it was an encouraging sign that Mortifer himself lived here at least some of the time.

Now we passed small utilitarian bedrooms, all empty. Some human staff must live here then, at least part of the time. Presently a few more pretentious bedrooms showed that Mortifer sometimes housed guests or had human servants to whom he allowed some luxuries.

We now reached a more elaborate door closing off the passage; our lock-opening machine took several minutes to solve the problem of opening it. Eventually the door flashed open and we entered a long, richly decorated corridor; there were soft carpets underfoot and paintings on the wall. As we went down the corridor at a trot a man in dark clothing emerged from a side room carrying a tray with dishes on it. A neural interrupter flashed and he dropped to the floor, but not before he had time to utter a warning cry into a disc on his wrist. I couldn't hear what he had yelled, of course, but it was probably enough to warn Mortifer.

I reached over my shoulder and pulled my sword from its sheath strapped to my back, and all of our party unslung fire-shields and held them at the ready. We went down the corridor at a trot, dashing past doors, as members of our party peeled off to deal with whatever the side rooms might contain.

The corridor ended in a circular anteroom from which three elaborate doors opened; solid doors hung on hinges—not the usual doors which flashed white and vanished to allow entrance. As we came to the anteroom some instinct made me halt my group. We waited, pressed against the corridor wall until the men who had fallen behind to deal with the side rooms joined us, signalling "All clear." The Healer touched me on the shoulder and handed me a little message square. In glowing letters on its surface I read, "Hidden speakers giving alarm. Have several times repeated sequence of nonsense syllables; may be your 'deathword.' "

I nodded and signaled for a very special member of our group; an andro with a highly unusual power source and very simple programming. It dashed out into the anteroom, headed for the center door. Flame flared from the ceiling and when the andro protected itself with an upflung shield, the floor under it flashed white and the andro dropped from sight into some pit or abyss below.

I grinned mirthlessly and waved some of our special equipment forward. A device which vibrated so intensely that I could feel it through the soles of my feet immobilized the floor, while heavy-duty torchers flared out to destroy the painted ceiling of the anteroom and the weapons hidden above it.

My voice sounding strange in my deadened ears, I said, "Squad Three, left door. Squad Four, right door. Squads One and Two through the center door with me. Go!"

We crossed the antechamber in a few bounds and fell on the doors. On each side of me I could hear the other squads battering on locked or barricaded doors, but the central door burst open as we threw our weight on it and we burst into a room very much like the pictures I had seen of Mortifer's laboratory at the Academy in Thorn.

Mortifer himself was seated on a thronelike chair with a console of contacts and flashing lights before him. Behind him a display screen showed us ourselves bursting into the room as if in a mirror. Mortifer's mouth moved but of course I could hear nothing. Then with his crooked smile on his face he touched a contact before him. The room shuddered and the floor pressed on my feet. The screen behind Mortifer showed the surface of the lake now, and a strange object breaking its surface. Suddenly I realized that this room in which we stood was part of some flying vehicle, in which Mortifer was trying to escape.

I stepped forward, sword at the ready and Mortifer smiled again. He pressed another contact and on the screen behind him, written in letters of fire appeared the words

AVAUNT FRANKENSTEIN!

My vision blurred, my knees buckled as I dropped to the floor dimly conscious that both heart and breath had ceased.

18. The Starship

I regained consciousness to find the Healer from my assault team tending over me. My head ached and my breathing was heavy and unnatural. I realized that my breathing was not under my control. "Relax a minute more," whispered the Healer, and I realized that he had turned on my sound receptors. "We had a program all set to defuse that reflex once it was triggered," murmured the Healer. "Give it a moment to operate and I can shut off the heart-lung field."

I realized that I was lying on a carpeted floor with a forest of legs around me; my two squads had surrounded me, sheltering me with their bodies. The floor under me vibrated as I remembered the transport disc vibrating on my first ride in one, when we had passed near the starship taking off. I heard Mortifer's voice over the heads of my men. "You may arrest me as much as you wish, monitor, but in a few minutes we will be on my starship and I think my defenses will hold you off until then. You had better lay down your weapons or my men will cut you down as soon as we are inside the cargo bay."

The leader of Squad One knelt by my side and whispered, "Any instructions, ser?"

Fighting the heavy involuntary breathing I whispered back, "Keep him talking . . . give up weapons if you must . . . drop a flamer near my hand . . ."

A great shadow darkened the sky above us and I could see that the giant transport disc which formed the "floor" of Mortifer's secret laboratory was floating up into an open cargo bay on the great black disc of a starship. I heard my squadleader talking as calmly as if he had been standing on the streets of Thorn, "Academician Mortifer, this will get you nowhere. Kidnapping aboard a starship is a Commonwealth offense. Our support team undoubtedly had you under observation and a U.C. ship will be dispatched after you from Thorn starport. You will be stopped before you can go Q and come back to face increased charges."

"Nothing on Carpathia can stop this ship or keep my ship from slipping away into quasi-space," snapped Mortifer. "Drop your weapons or my men will cut you down." The squad leader gave a quiet order and weapons rained down about me, one flamer dropping neatly into my open hand.

Under cover of this the Healer whispered, "We've killed the reflex; I'm turning off the field." My breathing became normal again, but I practiced breathing as shallowly as I could; I might have to play dead in hopes of seizing some opportunity later. I heard the ominous clang of the closing doors of the cargo bay and the hiss of air equalizing pressure.

I was still sheltered by my monitors when I heard a woman's voice from a direction that could only be on the floor of the cargo bay. "Everything all right, Councillor Mortifer?" the voice asked. I turned my head slowly and stealthily so that when my squads moved away my "dead" open eyes could see as much as possible.

"On my part, yes," said Mortifer's voice, "but what about yours? This starship isn't *Sceptre*!"

"The Tribune had *Sceptre* impounded," said the woman's voice. "We had to seize this trading ship to carry out your instructions to meet you here." The fascinating thing about that was that it was a lie; we had not been able to trace the ownership of any starship to Mortifer or his friends; I had never even heard of the starship *Sceptre*, much less given orders to impound her. Someone was playing Mortifer false; had some of his own folk revolted?

"Fool," snapped Mortifer, showing his usual stupidity about handling his subordinates. If that tale had been true the woman deserved commendation, not insults. "Fool," he repeated. "Nothing could have caught *Sceptre*, but you've trapped us on some lumbering trader which will be run down before we can slip into quasi-space."

"I assure you, Councillor, not a single starship will lift to pursue us," said the woman. "What do you want done with these monitors?"

"Over against that wall for the moment," said Mortifer and the squads of monitors filed off of the disc which held the laboratory, showing me a group of humans in support suits not unlike ours with heavy weapons trained on my monitors. The woman who had been speaking to Mortifer was evidently the pale, red-haired woman who stood not far from me. I saw that she too wore a monitor's uniform and remembered the woman monitor who had tricked Casmir Thorn into Mortifer's hands. "Freeze this body until I can get around to dissecting it," said Mortifer matter of factly. That gave me a little time; whatever move I made would have to be made before I went into the freezer. They would hardly be foolish enough to put me in it in my support suit; even turned off it would impede the quick-freeze action.

"Shall I intern the monitors in some of the crew rooms?" asked the red-haired woman.

"No," said Mortifer almost casually. "They are of no use to me. Cut them down."

The woman looked at him and became even paler. "Ser, I can't do that," she said.

"Can't!" said Mortifer. I half saw from the corner of my eye that he had risen from his console and was coming toward me. "You've disobeyed me for the last time, bitch. I'll torch you first and then cut the others down myself." He reached down for a flamer dropped by one of my monitors. With a roll and a bound I had him from behind; one of my arms around his throat and my sword point touching his neck just under his ear.

"Drop your weapons," I called to the red-haired woman and her followers. To my surprise they broke into broad grins and lowered their weapons immediately. A door flashed open behind them and a tall man accompanied by a dog came out of it. The dog was a ghost-hound, not Trinka but a younger dog, and I thought a male. The man had a face tanned by some fiercer sun than that of Carpathia, a scar on his forehead and a flamboyant blond mustache. But the eyes were my eyes and the grin my grin as he laid his hand on the ghost-hound's head and said, "Peace, my brother. I'm Casmir Thorn, and this piratical-looking bunch are my crew-mates on Starship *Argo*, in which you stand." The ghost-hound remained placidly white as he went on. "The lady with the fiery locks is our friend, Nadia Ivanovna, who had the courage to pretend to still be Mortifer's creature after she had changed her allegiance to me."

Our eyes met across the room; he knew as well as I the strength of the Jagellon Gift. "Our apologies for the mummery, but we had to lure Mortifer away from the controls of that thing you rode up here on; he could have done considerable damage to *Argo* from that console and he was shielded besides. The sword is probably not necessary, brother, but keep a good hold on Mortifer's throat; he may have a few other 'death-words' for you or me and I'd prefer not to find out the hard way. Nadia, my dear, if you would use a neural interrupter on Mortifer I doubt if you would do my brother any harm; I'm sure he is as full of Lysergol as I would be in his place."

Looking rather stunned, Nadia Ivanovna looked to me for permission and when I grinned at her and nodded, she pointed a familiar stubby weapon at Mortifer, who struggled frantically in my arms. There was a purple flash and he slumped, but I did not release him.

"Quite right, brother," said Casmir Thorn. "He might be faking. Nadia, a stasis suit for the distinguished Academician." The red-haired woman slipped a sort of gray shroud over Mortifer and two of my monitors took charge of him.

"We seem to have done it, brother," I said to Casmir Thorn.

He grinned. "With both of us against him, poor Mortifer had very little chance," he said. "Not to mention our allies. Gorda, go see if Mortifer is really fast asleep." The young ghost-hound padded over to where the shrouded Mortifer was held by the monitors, sniffed at him, yawned and sat down and scratched.

I laughed. "Mortifer seems to be no threat," I said. "I suppose Gorda is the replacement ghost-hound we ordered."

Casmir Thorn nodded. "I hope that you don't mind paying a rather high freight rate for him," he said. "My captain is a good friend but also a shrewd business woman. Gorda comes direct from Chrysonomia, the only planet where humans and Caphellans live together. I recommend that we each spend some time there."

I nodded thoughtfully; the ghost-hounds had renewed the interest in Caphellans which had been stirred by my first meeting with one. "They may have much to teach us," I agreed. I walked over to stand near Casmir Thorn, and both crew members and monitors withdrew respectfully, leaving us alone at one side of the cargo bay. "You've been on *Argo* since you destroyed Mortifer's laboratory in Thorn?" I asked.

"Oh, he did that himself to keep his secrets from falling into the hands of the mob that came to rescue me. I never learned that young scholar's name . . ." said Casmir Thorn.

"Paul Sobeski," I said. "He's my secretary now. If you had contacted him again, you might be Tribune now instead of me."

He shrugged. "Nadia got me out of the exploding laboratory and warned me about the deathword. Since I didn't know when Mortifer might spring that on me, it seemed safer to take up Captain Petros on an offer of a berth on *Argo*, leaving Nadia to work from within. But when I heard of an order for a Caphellan ghost-hound by Casmir King, Tribune of Carpathia, clone of King Casmir the Tenth . . ."

I laughed. "You didn't want to miss out on the end," I told him.

He laughed in his turn. "Of course not," he said. "And

just as well for you that I got here in time, contacted Nadia, and arranged to disable *Sceptre* and have *Argo* make the rendezvous. Of course, either of us alone might have done it, but as it was what you didn't do, I did . . ."

". . . And what you didn't do, I did," I finished. "Yes, that's something to be thought of for the future. Not that we always want to work together . . ."

"But we ought to duplicate experiences where possible," said Casmir Thorn. "I think I can persuade Captain Petros to train another green recruit when you can get away . . ."

". . . And you should have no trouble getting elected Tribune; the Jagellon legend is still very strong on Carpathia," I replied.

"Paul Sobeski and some others know about us, but we'll have to break the news of your existence to the people eventually."

"You'll need to meet a nurse named Molly and an ultraviolet named Benton—and his sister," said the other Casmir, "and we both need to consult with Justinian Droste."

"I've met Molly," I said, "and that reminds me our credit accounts are the same, unless Droste has taken steps to get it straightened out, and I don't think he has."

Casmir Thorn shrugged. "Leave it as it is, if they'll let us," he said. "Half of my pay as a starship crewman goes to Central Credit at Home, the other half I get in ecus. So we have credit at Home . . ."

". . . And plenty on Carpathia," I told him. "The Tribune's stipend is fairly modest, but I haven't had a chance to spend much of it."

"Good," said Casmir Thorn. "I've spent most of my ecus on artifacts from off-world . . ."

Just then a crewman approached us and said a little uncertainly, "Casmir?"

The other Casmir grinned and said, "We're both Casmir, Jogo, but he's only the Tribune of Carpathia and I'm the second supercargo of *Argo*."

"Aw well, we can't all be lucky," said the crewman with

perfect seriousness. "He looks just like you did when you came aboard. Anyway, Captain wants you both on the bridge. Says if you don't want to go right back to Thorn she wants to know who's paying for all this time on GE. In fact I guess she wants to know that anyway."

"I think I can answer that one," I said. "And I'd like to communicate with my backup crew, too. Will someone find my monitors somewhere to rest up?"

"Sure," said Jogo. "I'll take 'em to the crew lounge and give 'em a drink if they'll take it; we're not going Q anytime soon."

"Tell them from me that they're off duty except for the ones in charge of Mortifer," I said, "and they'll get their chance to celebrate later."

"Yesser," said Jogo and strode off with the catlike tread that seemed to be characteristic of starcrew.

The other Casmir chuckled. "You must have impressed him to get a 'ser,' " he said. "We starflitters rather look down on you planetaries."

Once back in Thorn Mortifer was handed over to Universal Commonwealth authorities; safer than trying to keep him on Carpathia where some of his secret sympathizers might work to free him. I requested the Council to reimburse Captain Elena Petros for all expenses incurred by *Argo* and to open the Lake of the Crater for swimming by local children as soon as possible. Such "requests" were increasingly mere formalities which worried me more than a little. I didn't mind being watchdog of Carpathia's liberties, but I had no desire to be her king.

It was late that night when all of the formalities were over and Casmir Thorn and I paced the battlements of Castle Thorn in the moonlight. Soberly I told Casmir Thorn of the last time I had seen a face like mine by moonlight.

"Needless to say, I would have done the same," he told me. "Our talents and Mortifer's mind was a combination just too dangerous to take any chances with."

"What are the limits of our talent?" I asked him. "Would

a man like Justinian Droste or a woman like Wanda Jagellon do something against their conscience because of the loyalty we inspire?''

He shook his head slowly. ''I hope not,'' he said. ''Otherwise the burden becomes almost too great to bear. Perhaps the Caphellans can help us find our limits—and our strengths. Will you flit when *Argo* lifts or shall I?''

''I'd better go this time,'' I said. ''Otherwise you'll be too far ahead of me in the crew hierarchy. You can stand for Tribune or not as you please; things are quiet now. You can live here in the castle in any case; the Knights are regarding us as co-Commanders, and the rooms go with that office, not with the Tribune's office.''

He nodded. ''Perhaps I'll wait and see,'' he said. ''We don't want to slip into being *de facto* kings and a rest from a Casmir as Tribune might help there. Besides, I want to explore some of the back country, see how much it has changed. No need for us to parallel exactly, so long as each keeps in touch with the other's experience.''

''Will we always parallel?'' I mused. ''Could we ever come into conflict?''

The other Casmir frowned thoughtfully. ''We're different men, that I know. I think, for one thing that you're more reflective than I and I'm more inclined to act before I think. I wish we had Mortifer's records; I suspect that our differences started even back in those identical environments. But of course we're far more like than unlike; closer than brothers, closer than twins. For better or worse we'll grow more unlike our prototype; *he* never had a parallel Casmir. As for whether you and I ever come into conflict I find it hard to imagine but I don't know.''

''If we do,'' I said, looking up at the stars, ''we can arrange that our paths don't cross at the same place at the same time. It's a big universe, big enough for . . . what can you call us? . . . a parallel man.''